QUENTIN TARANTINO'S "DEATH PROOF"

WEINSTEIN BOOKS

ISBN: 978-1-60286-009-4
ISBN 10: 1-60286-009-2

First Edition
10 9 8 7 6 5 4 3 2 1

"DEATH PROOF"

INTRODUCTION

It's probably not the best way to get to know a screenplay, having it read to you by its author. Then again, maybe it is; hearing Quentin Tarantino read the pages aloud in big, raw chunks, oozing vitality and intimacy, was a telling and unique introduction to the population of *Death Proof*—even the car had a life of its own, and not just in the KITT 2000 sense either. Tarantino's own admiration for the characters came with awe because his reading demonstrated how each of the creations took on a self-involved, argumentative life of their own; all of them swinging elbows to make room for themselves in the conversation, anxiously needing to be heard, competing for every single breath and syllable. The way he depicted the women, changing the rhythms of their talk, expressing their individual concerns and looking for a place in their circle, had the kind of dense, teeming surprise of drama. Especially for me, because I was getting to hear them as they were being invented, screaming and clawing their way into a world that became increasingly more unsure for all of them. Because a mounting sense of dread materialized with each scene.

I'm not entirely sure how he put *Death Proof* together. Sure, I knew that he wrote the pages by hand—everyone understands the rudiments of his process by now; you'd be hard-pressed to find a coffee shop, public library or backseat of a station wagon in Southern California where screenwriters-manqué aren't aping his low-tech D.I.Y. scribbling, hunched over legal pads and English composition notebooks in ways that will produce kinks and muscle strains some Westside chiropractor will eventually have to beat and adjust out of them as they're trying to reproduce Tarantino™ sweat and caffeine stains in their own work; the film version of pre-distressed Martin Margiela shoes. A few of these films even see fruition. But the fascinating thing about hearing him read the pages aloud is how each of the characters has something very specific at stake—in most of the cases, a hunger to be understood in their own terms. The tribal rites, with each group featuring a couple of folks sniffing, scratching and pissing to mark alpha dog territory was made immediately evident to me being so close to the author himself and the distance between him and his imitators was suddenly like the gap between Al Green and Ruben Studdard; it's what separates talent from inspiration. I initially encountered this when I ran into Tarantino at the 2004 Sitges Film Festival, where I was on the jury and he was a guest. Having just finished a meal and chat with Johnnie To, he came over and we greeted each other. He then began telling me about the script he was writing—a conversation that, in what I learned was typical Tarantino fashion, quickly became digressive rather than discursive. The talk bounced from the script to festival attendee Takashi Miike, was spiked into a slam about plans for several other projects he wanted to do and volleys into several other areas before crossing the net near where we started. "Do you mind if I read something?" he said and reached into the sheaf of papers on the table. Expecting to get scenes from his new script, and wondering how close it would sound to what I suspected his stuff does at an inchoate stage, I was treated to something altogether different. What I heard turned out to be reviews for a compendium of writings on film that he had in mind, an undertaking that I hope he completes soon. Weeks later, he called and said, "Would it be OK if I read you something?" This something ended up being pages from *Death Proof,* which he never got around to letting me hear before.

All of this was instructive because witnessing the way Tarantino conducts himself can aid in understanding the genesis of his movies; he leads his life as if it were a series of subplots, and just when you've been distracted by a new and emerging circumstance, he returns—sometimes impatiently, sometimes gracefully—to the subject at hand. In the films themselves, this is accomplished in equally distinctive ways, occasionally obvious and others, far more subtle; the segues are handled in a manner like, oh, a sleight of hand artist practicing prestidigitation (*Pulp Fiction*) or like a summer breeze shifting direction and intensity (*Jackie Brown*) or a series of memories violently triggered (the *Kill Bill* films). And although *Death Proof* more or less takes place in a more or less straightforward linear fashion, its teeming with the shifting psychological points of view give the script that same sense of fluidity as his other movies, while linking up with the drive-in films, in which point of view traveled adroitly from one character to another with a spirit that was part c'mon-let's-get-on-with-it and part let's-get-it-out, a freewheeling need to try out the daring as the clock burns up time, money and the audience's attention span. There's an unapologetic lack of shame—and, yes, taste—that fuels the exploitation films that are much a point of departure for Tarantino as Sam Fuller and Jean-Luc Godard.

All of the other influences aside, finally, it's all about intensity in Tarantino's scripts and he invests each moment with such passion as it unfolds that each beat demands attention all its own. I don't have a great deal of experience reading scripts—which is why it helped to listen to him going through the pages, and frankly, the incomplete state of the script at the time demanded that he do so—and when I do, I'm reminded of Paul Schrader's line about screenwriters: he said a screenwriter isn't a writer, he's half a filmmaker, and that screenplays are in effect schematic drawings of what they hope will be accomplished by the director. It is, Schrader said, why screenwriters become filmmakers. With Tarantino's work, it's hard to imagine anybody directing what he's written because it's important for him to convey the rhythm of scenes as they happen—that beating of the heart, changing as his characters rev up and downshift into cruise control, apparently listening to each other but not really; actually, they're almost all waiting for a chance to talk. Often, it's like Popeye in those beautiful black and white Fleischer Studios cartoons, talking to himself if no one is going to hear them.

The phenomenon of watching Tarantino read pages from his scripts isn't exactly like having a holographic version of the script leap conjured before your very eyes, but you actually hear what the movie could be. It's not a big leap to imagine how he's going to direct the script; Schrader's dictum about the screenplay being the schematic makes perfect sense. It's clearer than ever as Tarantino reads the pages that his films don't take place in a vacuum—the sense of community is undeniable, and central to the conception because the characters actually live someplace. It's mostly been Los Angeles and in *Death Proof*, it's Austin, Texas, which is an amalgam of college town, music magnet and laid-back dreamscape, since it's entirely possible that the person sitting in the banquette behind you eavesdropping on your conversation and interrupting to correct you could be Robyn Hitchcock, or Questlove? Or Quentin Tarantino. Rather than desperation, which can make anyone—and I mean anyone—in Los Angeles feel like you've made the wrong decision, Austin's floating sense of anything-can-happen, and the inviting, hyper-voluble Texan friendliness that can take a wrong turn if too many tequilas have been downed are part of the ambience in *Death Proof*.

Of course, there was an extra added element of fun in *Death Proof*. That is, hearing Tarantino read all of the girls' chatter; his glee over the women as he went through their speeches—and in their own specific way, the girl talk shows that the women are just as territorial over conversation and claiming ideas as the guys he's written—made me believe that he's known them. As much getting a chance to spin his boys'-club reputation on its head, I could hear the excitement as he served up dialogue that showed how much time he's spent sitting around listening to women and soaking up their attitudes and cadences, too. Maybe his greatest gift as a screenwriter is that complete immersion in loving to hear people talk, particularly people who have enormous confidence in expressing themselves verbally, part Robert Towne, part Chester Himes and part Patricia Highsmith.

After having had sections of the *Death Proof* screenplay read to me—and being caught up enough in it every time that it only occurred to me after each occasion that he didn't bother to try and do a "voice" for each of the characters, but read them straight as if he were auditioning for the roles— I honestly was a little nervous when he offered to give me a copy of the finished version. I dug the cliffhanger aspect of it, and how he'd leap into every new portion without preamble, convinced that his conviction in the writing would bring me right up to speed. I was concerned, too, that his energy level and force of personality might have inflated the whole thing. I wasn't standing over his shoulder to check what he was reading, and he is a born entertainer as much as anything else. So, I put my shoulder to the task, sitting at a hotel patio on an unusually gray day in Los Angeles. And I was instantly so pulled into the backbeat of the story, the hilarious and innocuous squabblings, the offhanded menace that took bracing turns into horror and the sheer, bounding recklessness of it all that I hadn't noticed the sun had burned through the clouds and I sat in pools of sweat. Also, I'd let a rare and very expensive pre-Castro Cuban Henry Clay cigar go cold—something I'll never forgive myself, or Mr. Tarantino, for. But the investment in the dialogue, as well as the cold-hearted efficiency of the action on the pages—action that offers as much plot development as the dialogue, since reactions, and reaction time as well, define character—made the *Death Proof* screenplay seem compact, rather than distended. A few lines and beats that I liked were lost, but discarded because the drag time they brought into play robbed the final effort of its streamlined quality. As I mentioned, I'm not a fan of reading screenplays—because often, I think Schrader is right, there's something missing from them that it can be tough to supply or they can be overwritten and overwhelming in their underestimation of the reader. After having the screenplay directed as it was read aloud, I felt I'd seen the movie already. But the weight, fumes and velocity of *Death Proof* was something I hadn't counted on. The rough, beaten beauty was only enhanced once I went through it, and I was just as entertained and shocked by the climax as I was when I heard it. It was multiplied by its completion. Bravo, Mr. Tarantino—now, about that cigar you owe me.

—Elvis Mitchell, host of the
interview show *The Treatment*

"Death Proof"

Written

by

Quentin Tarantino

Final Draft
Valentine's Day
2006

This script is dedicated
to the poet laureate of
The Drive-in
CHARLES B. GRIFFITH
Your work has always
"Rocked All Night," daddy-o.

Respect,

Quentin Tarantino

POV OF A CAR WINDSHIELD—DAY

The car is driving fast down the road. A pair of
female bare feet with a gold ankle bracelet lie
propped up on the dashboard emanating from the
passenger seat.

A Good God Almighty rockabilly tune beats out of the
car stereo; the feet tap to the beat.

The opening credits play out over this image.

As the music continues

WE CUT TO:

INT. JUNGLE JULIA'S APARTMENT—DAY

A tall (maybe 6 foot) Amazonian mulatto goddess walks
down her hallway, dressed in a baby tee, and panties
that her big ass (a good thing) spill out of and her
long legs grow out of. Her big bare feet slap on the
hard wood floor. She moves to the cool rockabilly beat
as she paces like a tiger putting on her clothes.

Outside her apartment she hears a "honk honk."

She sticks her long mane of silky black, curly hair, her
giraffish neck, and her broad shoulders out of the window
and yells down to a car below.

This sexy chick is Austin, Texas, local celebrity
JUNGLE JULIA LUCAI, the most popular disc jockey of
the coolest rock radio station in a music town.

                    JUNGLE JULIA
          I'm comin' down!

EXT. STREET OUTSIDE JULIA'S APARTMENT—DAY

Two girls are getting out of a white Honda Civic
that's parked across the street from Jungle Julia's
apartment.

One girl is SHANNA...

The other (the one with the sexy opening credit feet)
is ARLENE.

All three girls are in their three-years-after-college
phase.

The dynamic of the trio is that Julia, Shanna, and
Arlene all went to the University of Texas together.

Shanna being a Texas native, Corpus Christi to be exact.

Julia being from Austin.

Arlene being from Brooklyn.

After school was over, Arlene went back to New York, Julia got into the local Austin music scene, becoming a fixture on the scene, and ultimately becoming a drive-time D.J. for the local oldies radio station Austin Hot Wax 505, and in the process turning into one of the most popular local celebrities since Stevie Ray Vaughn.

Arlene's in town visiting for a week, and it's sorta fallen on Shanna to take care of her.

But since Julia's become a celebrity in the meantime, every plan, arrangement, and girls' night out is vaguely catered around Julia.

As Julia screams down to them, Arlene hurries across the street and screams up to her in her thick Brooklyn accent.

> ARLENE
> (yelling up)
> Hold on, I gotta come up! I gotta take the world's biggest fuckin' piss!

> JUNGLE JULIA
> (yelling down)
> We can't be late!

> SHANNA
> (yelling up)
> We won't!

As Arlene and Shanna hurry up the stairs to Julia's apartment, the rockabilly on the soundtrack is cut off (by a needle being lifted), and a different song is put on the soundtrack.

INT. JUNGLE JULIA'S APARTMENT—DAY

Julia has just put on a new record and is dancing to the music.

Arlene enters the front door with "I gotta pee" body language.

Julia points in the direction of the bathroom.

Arlene disappears behind the bathroom door.

Shanna and Julia dance to the record while Arlene
pees.

INT. BATHROOM—DAY

Arlene is sitting on the toilet; a racehorse stream of
piss can be heard emanating from under her. We slowly
zoom into the pretty face of relief.

EXT. JUNGLE JULIA'S APARTMENT—DAY

In slow motion, the three girls walk out of the
apartment and head for their car.

They climb into Shanna's car and head off to their
next exciting 3 girls 3 adventures.

As the Honda drives away, A SUBTITLE APPEARS BELOW:

                    The City of
                    Austin, Texas

INT. HONDA (MOVING)—DAY

Shanna is behind the wheel, Arlene is in the passenger
seat, and Jungle Julia lies sprawled out in the
backseat, her feet out the car door window, like
Cleopatra.

                    JUNGLE JULIA
          Who's holding?

                    SHANNA
          If you're not, then nobody.

Arlene turns around in her seat to talk to the lying
down Julia.

                    ARLENE
          We were kinda hoping you were.

                    SHANNA
          Yeah, how are you not holding?

                    JUNGLE JULIA
          Jesus Christ, Shanna, it's not my
          fucking job to supply weed to y'all
          when we go out.

SHANNA
Whoa whoa whoa, little lady, you're
getting angry kinda quick, don'tcha
think? I was just teasing you.

JUNGLE JULIA
I'm not angry; it would just be
nice if y'all didn't just count on
me all the fuckin' time, and
surprised me every once in a while
with pot.

SHANNA
Okay, mean girl in a high school
movie, are you through being angry?

JUNGLE JULIA
I'm not angry.

SHANNA
Yes, you are, you've been in the
car all of two seconds, and you're
already cursing at me.

JUNGLE JULIA
I'm not cursing at you.

SHANNA
You said, "Jesus-Christ-Shanna."
And before the sentence was over,
you threw a "fuckin'" in there to
emphasize your irritatedness.

Julia smiles; she's not really mad anymore. Arlene
takes it a little too seriously.

ARLENE
C'mon, guys, don't fight. I'll pay
for it when we get some.

JUNGLE JULIA
One, it's not about the money, it's
about the pain in the ass of
scoring, and two, we're not really
fighting.

SHANNA
Arlene, you've forgotten what
hanging out with Jungle Julia's
like. That wasn't a fight. That was
Julia acting like a grumpy bitch
and me calling her on it and
indulging her at the same time.

                    SHANNA
        It's how we tolerate each other
        after all these years.

                    JUNGLE JULIA
        Oh, yeah, like you're never a
        bitch.

                    SHANNA
        Oh, yeah, like you're never not.

They both bust out laughing. Arlene guesses it's okay,
and joins along.

                    SHANNA
        So what's the plan, man?

                    JUNGLE JULIA
        Margaritas and Mexican food at
        Güero's — did you call Rafael, tell
        him we're comin'?

                    SHANNA
        Of course.

                    JUNGLE JULIA
        You're so good.

                    SHANNA
        I know. Okay, is Christian Simonson
        going to be there?

Julia smiling.

                    JUNGLE JULIA
        You bet your ass he is. He's gonna
        be there with Jessie Letterman.

Shanna to Arlene.

                    SHANNA
        Christian Simonson the filmmaker is
        in town. And he's got a big thing
        for Julia.

                    JUNGLE JULIA
        If he had a big thing for me, he'd
        fuckin' call me as opposed to
        disappearing for six months. And
        he'd get his ass down here more
        often then he does, and on my
        birthday he'd give me a fucking
        phone call. But other than that,
        he's putty in my hands.

                    SHANNA
        Yeah, but you get those legs of
        yours around him, it's all over.
                 (to Arlene)
        Chris has got a thing for long
        Amazonian legs, and so whenever we
        hang out, eventually Julia will get
        her legs around Chris, or across
        him, and when she does, Chris ain't
        going nowhere. And neither is she.

                  JUNGLE JULIA
        Yeah, well, when I'm redecorating
        his house in the hills that I'm
        also living in, I'll let you know
        it worked. So, margaritas and
        Mexican food at Güero's. Touch base
        with Chris and Jessie, tell them
        about later, and make damn sure
        they come. The other guys'll be
        waiting for us to join them at
        Huck's.
                 (to Arlene)
        Oh shit, speaking of which, what
        happened with you and Nate last
        night?

Arlene starts to recount last night's hookup with her
tough girl way of talking.

                    ARLENE
        Well, not much, you know, we just
        fuckin' met each other. I mean, if
        you don't bust their balls a little
        bit, they never gonna respect ya'.

                  JUNGLE JULIA
        Okay, we're pretty clear on what
        you didn't do. How 'bout
        enlightening us on what you did do?

                    ARLENE
        Awww, nothin' to write home about;
        we just made out on the couch for
        about twenty minutes.

                    SHANNA
        Dressed, half-dressed, or naked?

                    ARLENE
        Dressed. I said we made out; we
        didn't do "the thing."

                    JUNGLE JULIA
          Excuse me for livin', but what's
          "the thing"?

                    ARLENE
          You know, everything but.

                    SHANNA
          They call that "the thing"?

                    ARLENE
          I call it "the thing."

                    SHANNA
          Do guys like "the thing"?

                    ARLENE
          Well, they like it better than
          no-thing.

The girls laugh.

                    JUNGLE JULIA
          Okay, I wanna get back to what it
          is you did do? So you're making out
          with Nate on the couch, right?

                    ARLENE
          Correct.

                    JUNGLE JULIA
          Whose couch, his or the one in your
          hotel room?

                    ARLENE
          What am I, stupid over here, mine.

                    SHANNA
          Were you making out sitting up, or
          lying down?

                    ARLENE
          Started sitting up, worked our way
          to lying down.

                    JUNGLE JULIA
          Hummm, the plot gets thicker. Who
          was on top?

                    ARLENE
          I was straddlin' him.

SHANNA
(to Jungle Julia)
Oh, you know Nate had to love that.
What else?

ARLENE
Well, not much; that was it. So we
made out a little while on the
couch, and I say, "Okay, I'm gonna
go to bed, so it's time for you to
leave." And then he whines, "Awww,
right now?" And I say, "Yep, right
now, let's go." Then he says, "Wait
a minute, how 'bout this?" And I
say, "No." And he says, "What'd you
mean no? You don't even know what
I'm gonna say." And I say, "I
already know what you're gonna
say. . .
(beat)
...and the answer's no." And he
says, "How can you say, you know
what I'm gonna say?" And I say,
"Because you're gonna say, let's
just go to bed together — we don't
gotta do nothin' — just cuddle —
sleep next to each other — wake up
in the morning together —
(beat)
No.
(beat)
You're gonna leave.
(beat)
But I'll see you tomorrow."

SHANNA
So what about tonight?

ARLENE
Well, we'll see. Look, I like Nate.
He's cute, he's a nice guy, he's a
pretty good kisser...but,...
it ain't a done deal.

JUNGLE JULIA
Yeah, fuck Nate. I mean, yeah, he's
cute an all, but Jessie Letterman's
gonna be all over her.

ARLENE
Jessie Letterman, the Austin
director who did "Potheads"?

                    JUNGLE JULIA
          He's a good friend.

                    ARLENE
          Remember freshman year, getting
          stoned and going to the Dobie to
          see "Potheads"?

                    JUNGLE JULIA
          Just think, play your cards right,
          you'll be sucking his dick within
          hours.

The girls laugh.

                    SHANNA
          Hey, Jessie's got a big dick.

                    ARLENE
          You sucked Jessie Letterman's dick?

                    JUNGLE JULIA
          Half the girls in Austin have
          sucked Jessie's dick.

                    SHANNA
          Yeah, but don't get your hopes up
          too high. Christian and Jessie
          might not even show up; they're big
          flakes.

                    JUNGLE JULIA
          I'll kick his ass he doesn't show
          up.

                    SHANNA
          But remember, we're not hooking up
          tonight. We're gonna hang out at
          Huck's with 'em, you can make out
          with 'em, but no hookin' up, cause
          we're driving to Lake LBJ tonight,
          and my daddy's pretty clear about
          one thing. He said, "I'm letting
          you and your girlfriends stay at my
          lake cabin. Not you and a buncha
          horny boys tryin' to get their fuck
          on with my daughter."

                    ARLENE
          Your dad talks like that?

Julia and Shanna say together:

                    JULIA/SHANNA
Hell, yeah!

                    SHANNA
It's not like he ain't gonna know
either. Because when I'm stayin' at
the cabin with my girlfriends, in
our bikinis, Daddy has a tendency
to just pop up, and make sure we
don't need anything.

They all laugh.

                    SHANNA
Look, he's totally harmless and cute
as a bug's ear, but when he's got a
bunch of half-naked poontang walkin'
the floor of his cabin, he just likes
to pay a visit and make sure we got
everything we need. And if you flirt
shamelessly with him like the six
foot baby giraffe in the backseat,
you've got a puppy dog for life.

                    JUNGLE JULIA
I have my own relationship with Ben,
and you're just jealous, because it
doesn't include you.

                    ARLENE
You call her dad Ben?

                    JUNGLE JULIA
I'm not a child, and that's his
name.

                    ARLENE
Where's this bar we're going to
later?

                    SHANNA
Huck's.

                    JUNGLE JULIA
It's a dive, but a fucking cool
dive.

                    SHANNA
Yeah, no more college kid Sixth
Street bullshit. Huck's is about
drinking booze. No cosmos, nothing
with a blender, just beers, booze,
and shots.

                    JUNGLE JULIA
And great music; don't forget about
the music.

                    SHANNA
Yeah, Warren, the guy who owns the
place, has this great classic
jukebox. He calls it Amy.

                    ARLENE
He's got a classic jukebox that
plays CDs?

                    JUNGLE JULIA
No! That's what's so cool about it,
dummy. It's filled with classic Stax
and Decca 45s. They have moonshine
under the counter.

                    SHANNA
Yeah,
  (and with a thick southern accent)
And that shine'll blind ya', boy.
You order coffee and he puts it in
the coffee.

                    JUNGLE JULIA
And Cabo Wabo tequila.

Arlene's trying to forget Julia just called her a dummy
two seconds ago. She could be the hurt girl or the cool
dude chick, and has decided in her last two days in
Texas to be the dude chick.

                    ARLENE
What's Cabo Wabo?

                    JUNGLE JULIA
Sammy Hagar, The Red rocker's own
personal brand of tequila.

                    ARLENE
When are the boys showing up?

                    JUNGLE JULIA
We're gonna meet them at Huck's.

                    ARLENE
Maybe they can bring some pot.

                    JUNGLE JULIA
          Fuck those guys. I don't want to be
          either, A, depending on their
          fucking ass, or B, dependent on
          their ass. If we don't score
          ourselves, we're going to be stuck
          with them all fucking night.

                    SHANNA
          Try Lanna-Frank.

                    JUNGLE JULIA
          Best idea you've had all day.

Julia takes out her cell phone, pushes one button.

                    JUNGLE JULIA
          Lanna-Frank?
                    (pause)
          Julia.
                    (pause)
          Hey girl.
                    (pause)
          Is <u>Steve</u> with you?
                    (pause)
          Yes!
                    (to the other girls)
          Steve's with her.
                    (back to Lanna-Frank)
          Look, Shanna and I and our friend
          from out of town, Arlene, are going
          to Güero's now and then Huck's
          later. Maybe you could meet us at
          either one of those places, and if
          <u>Steve's</u> around, bring him along.

"Steve" is obviously these girls' idea of a secret
code for pot.

                    JUNGLE JULIA
                    (pause)
          So...you're thinking, midnightish?
                    (pause)
          Now don't flake out, bitch, we're
          counting on you.
                    (pause)
          Bye.
                    (she hangs up and
                    looks to the other
                    girls)
          Mission accomplished.

                    SHANNA
          Hey, we're passing by your
          billboard.

                    JUNGLE JULIA
          Oh c'mon, give me a break.

                    SHANNA
          C'mon my ass, we said every time.

                    JUNGLE JULIA
          Okay.

Julia rises to sitting position.

EXT. TEXAS ROAD—DUSK

A billboard of Jungle Julia Lucai, the disc jockey of
the local classic rock station Austin Hot Wax 505. The
billboard shows Julia dressed as a leopard-spotted Julia
of the Jungle, a Tarzan type surrounded by stacks of
records.

Different styles of Jungle Julia billboards are all
over town.

As the girls pass by it they scream.

...they pass by down the road...

...empty road, just billboard...

...then a menacing-looking muscle car with a powerful
thumping engine...passes by.

INT. MUSCLE CAR (MOVING)—DUSK

Out of the windshield of the powerful, scary muscle
car. Trailing the girls from way far back.

The unseen DRIVER's eyes, hidden behind dark glasses,
glance up at Jungle Julia's billboard as they pass it.

A bluesy, early seventies rock tune plays out of his
thumping speakers.

All we can see of the driver is that he wears a silver
satin jacket with an embroidered "ICY HOT" patch on
the back, wears his hair in a greasy, half-assed
pompadour, and smokes Chesterfields like a chimney, as
indicated by the overflowing ashtray.

As the music plays, we see various INSERTS of the dash of this mechanical monster, including one of the car keys in the ignition with a spark plug keychain.

His hood ornament is a muscle-bound duck flexing.

INT. THROUGH WINDSHIELD (MOVING)—DUSK

The girls have stopped in front of the Mexican restaurant Güero's and are piling out of the car.

His heavy boot eases off the gas pedal.

We see the arrow on the speedometer fall to a crawl.

OVER THE DRIVER'S SHOULDER

looking out the passenger-side window, we see the girls bullshitting as they walk from car to front door.

DRIVER'S POV

SLOW MOTION shot of all the girls and each one individually.

Each girl's Christian name and first initial of her last name appears beside each girl during her slow motion single.

JUNGLE JULIA L.

SHANNA S.

ARLENE M.

We see, rubber-banded to the sun visor, a Polaroid of Jungle Julia, Shanna, and Arlene, wearing different clothes. This stalking is not random. He didn't just find them today. This is one part of a longer process.

CU THE DRIVER

Just as the music reaches a crescendo, we cut to a tight Sergio Leone CU of the Driver, smiling...then...

...the badass vehicle speeds off, making a thunderous racket.

EXT. GÜERO'S—DUSK

Julia and Shanna, oblivious, walk into the restaurant. But something makes Arlene stop and give the muscle car an investigative gaze, as it hauls ass down the road.

Like "the final girl" in a slasher film, her look says: "Something's not right. But that's just silly." She shrugs it off and enters the restaurant to catch up with her friends.

INT. GÜERO'S—NIGHT

The three ladies sit at a big booth, post dinner, the dirty dishes have been taken away, but the table still shows the mess the girls made.

Shanna pours out the last of the margarita from their last pitcher.

The bill comes, already paid by Jungle Julia.

                    ARLENE
          Julia. You and Shanna have been
          paying for everything.

                    JUNGLE JULIA
          Hey, my town, my rules. But when I
          come to New York to visit you, I
          don't pay for shit.

                    ARLENE
          Deal. I mean, in that case we won't
          be doing a bunch of shit, but the
          shit we do do, deal.

While they went back and forth about the check. Shanna's phone rang; she's answered it, talked, and hung up.

                    SHANNA
          That's Omar and Nate and them;
          they're at the Huck's.

Jungle Julia whips out her cell phone and dials Christian Simonson's number. His voice mail picks up, and an outgoing message that Chris made while sitting at the Hemingway bar in the St. Regis hotel in Paris. In fact, you can hear Colin, the bartender, explaining a drink in the background.

                    CHRIS (VO)
          This is Chris,...leave a message.

Julia leaves her message.

                              JUNGLE JULIA
                             (into phone)
                    Okay, you didn't make Güero's, but
                    that's okay, I expected that. But
                    we're leaving for Huck's right now.
                    It would be a wonderful surprise if
                    you beat us there. But in any case
                    I'll see you in the next few hours.
                    Don't disappoint me.

Julia puts away her cell phone.

Shanna picks up her drink and proposes a toast with
their last margarita before moving on to Huck's.

Suddenly standing next to the table is a pretty, young
lady named MARCY.

Marcy and Julia know each other, and Julia stands up,
hugs and greets her. By the way, this is a normal
occurrence in Austin for Jungle Julia. People are always
coming up and saying hi, because she knows everybody.

Julia introduces her to the table.

                              JUNGLE JULIA
                    This is Marcy.
                             (re: Arlene)
                    This is a friend from Shanna and
                    I's U.T. days, Arlene.

They smile at each other.

                              JUNGLE JULIA
                    Want to join us?

                              MARCY
                    For a second, but I'm with some
                    friends.

                              JUNGLE JULIA
                    We're on our way out anyway.

Marcy joins them, sitting next to Julia, at the table.

                              JUNGLE JULIA
                             (to Marcy)
                    What are your plans tonight?

                    MARCY
          We're going to see the GoGo's at
          Stubb's, y'all goin'?

                    JUNGLE JULIA
          No. Maybe if it was 1982.

Marcy looks across the table at Arlene, then says:

                    MARCY
          So you must be the infamous
          Butterfly.

Julia and Shanna immediately go: SHHHHHH.

                    SHANNA
          She don't know nothin' about it.

                    ARLENE
          Know about what?

                    MARCY
          When were you gonna tell her?

                    SHANNA
          Soon.

                    ARLENE
          Tell me what?

                    JUNGLE JULIA
          Yeah, and now, thanks to you, we
          hafta tell her sooner than later.

                    ARLENE
               (Brooklyn accent coming on
               strong)
          Okay, cut the shit, what the fuck
          is goin' on?

                    JUNGLE JULIA
          Chill out, Barbarino. If you
          listened to my show this morning,
          you'd know.

                          ARLENE
          I know, honey, I'm sorry. I slept
          in this morning — we been stayin'
          out so fuckin' late every night,
          but I'm sorry I missed it.

                       JUNGLE JULIA
          Get a sense of humor, lady, I'm
          just kidding. Of course we been
          staying out late, and of course
          you're gonna sleep in. You were a
          sweetheart to get up and listen to
          it for the last few days. But I
          predicted you'd start getting sick
          of it today and sleep in. So that's
          why I said a little somethin' —
          somethin' about you — on the air
          today.

With dread creeping into her voice:

                          ARLENE
          Oh my God, what did you say?

                          SHANNA
          First off, she didn't use your real
          name, she used your code name.

                          ARLENE
          I don't have a code name.

                          MARCY
          You do now.

All three say in unison to Arlene.

                        ALL THREE
          Hey, Butterfly.

                          SHANNA
          C'mon, you can't tell me you don't
          like the name Butterfly. That's a
          pretty name.

                          ARLENE
          Julia, what the fuck did you say
          about me on the radio?

                    JUNGLE JULIA
          All I said was, I had a sexy friend
          of mine, named Butterfly, who was in
          from outta town this weekend, and
          we were going out somewhere in
          Austin tonight. And if they were
          out on the town, maybe they'd see
          us, and I described you. And I said
          if they spotted you while we were
          out, if they'd do something, you'd
          do something.

                       ARLENE
          Okay, now, Julia, I'm serious. What
          did you say, and what did you say I'd
          do?

                    JUNGLE JULIA
          Anywho, I could explain what I
          said, which would be boring, or
          Marcy, who is an incredible
          actress, could act it out for you.
          Which I think will give you a
          better idea about what you're in
          store for tonight.

                       ARLENE
          Just tell me.

Jungle Julia grabs her friend's hand and says;

                    JUNGLE JULIA
          I'm a raconteur. Honey, ya' gotta
          let me do my thing.

                       ARLENE
          Okay, I know, I know. Tell me your
          way.

                    JUNGLE JULIA
          So we'll act it out with Marcy?

                       ARLENE
          Sure.

                    JUNGLE JULIA
          Okay, give Marcy your drink.

Arlene slides her margarita over to Marcy, who now has
two.

> JUNGLE JULIA
> So you're in a club or a bar, and
> Marcy's a kinda cute, or kinda hot,
> or kinda sexy, or better be fuckin'
> hysterically funny, but not funny-
> looking, guy who you <u>could</u> fuck.

Arlene salutes.

> ARLENE
> Got it.

> JUNGLE JULIA
> Okay, Marcy, take it.

Marcy stands up and reapproaches the table, acting all
cool guy approaching a girl.

> MARCY
> (dude voice)
> Hey.

Arlene busts out laughing.

Jungle Julia interrupts.

> JUNGLE JULIA
> C'mon, grow up, stay in the moment.
> This ain't improv; you don't get
> points for breaking the scene.

> ARLENE
> Okay, sorry.
> (to Marcy)
> Hi there.

> MARCY
> Excuse me, but your name wouldn't
> be Butterfly, would it?

> ARLENE
> (all flirty)
> Yes it is, and it seems you have me
> at a disadvantage.

Marcy extends her hand like a him.

> MARCY
> Barry.

Arlene folds her hand femininely into Marcy's hand.

ARLENE
Pleased to meet you, Barry.

SHANNA
Y'all are getting me hot.

They both turn to Shanna and say: SHHHHHH!

The two girls turn back to each other and pick it up
again.

MARCY
Is Butterfly your real name?

She nods her head yes.

ARLENE
Yes, it is, and how did you know my
name, Barry?

MARCY
I listened to Jungle Julia's show
this morning.

ARLENE
Oh you did, did you?

MARCY
Oh yeah, I listen to her show every
morning.

ARLENE
Oh you do, do you?

MARCY
Yeah, she's the coolest lady in
town.

Arlene leans in, and says confidentially:

ARLENE
Don't you think she's got a big
ass?

MARCY
No, I like her ass that way. She's
got a black girl's ass.

                              ARLENE
          You know that's what she always
          says, but in actual fact, she
          doesn't really have a black girls
          ass, she's just got a big ass.

Using both of her hands spread wide for emphasis,
Julia interrupts —

                          JUNGLE JULIA
          Okay, what the fuck are you doing?

                              ARLENE
          Oh, look who wants to get to the
          point all of a sudden.

                          JUNGLE JULIA
          Okay, we'll get to the point. But
          just for your information, skinny-
          bitch, black men and a whole lotta
          motherfuckin' white men have had
          plenty fun adoring my ass. I don't
          wear their teeth marks in my butt
          for nothing.

Shanna laughs and raises up her hand.

                              SHANNA
          You gotta give me some on that one.

Shanna and Julia high five.

                              ARLENE
          If you're not going to buy me a
          drink, can I have mine back?

                              MARCY
          Okay okay okay.
                    (in character)
          So, Butterfly, can I buy you a
          drink?

                              ARLENE
                    (in character)
          That would be nice, Barry.

                              MARCY
          What can I get you?

                              ARLENE
          I'd love a margarita.

She slides it over.

> JUNGLE JULIA
> Here ya' go.

Marcy raises her glass to toast. Arlene does too; then
Jungle Julia, like the narrator of a novel, joins in
dramatically.

> JUNGLE JULIA
> (breaking character)
> So after they buy you a drink, when
> they raise their glass to toast,
> they look you dead in the eye, and
> repeat this poem:
>   "The woods are lovely
>   dark and deep
>   And I have promises to keep
>   And miles to go before I sleep."
> Did you hear me, Butterfly, miles to
> go before you sleep...and then
> ...if he says that...you gotta give
> him a lap dance.

> ARLENE
> What!

> JUNGLE JULIA
> If they call you Butterfly, buy you
> a drink, and say that poem, you
> gotta give 'em a lap dance.

> ARLENE
> That's bullshit. I ain't givin'
> them nothin'.

> JUNGLE JULIA
> Look, you can do it or not. But if
> you don't do it, everybody in
> Austin's gonna think you're a
> chicken shit, and I don't think you
> want everybody in Austin thinkin'
> you're a chicken shit.

> ARLENE
> I ain't givin' nobody no lap dance
> cause of what you said.

> SHANNA
> It's gonna be funny.

> ARLENE
> Yeah, everything's funny to you two
> when it's happening to me.

                    JUNGLE JULIA
         Be that as it may, — look, you don't
         have to do it with anybody you don't
         want. I said you'll do it for the
         first guy who says it. So some geek
         comes over and tries to be cool, just
         tell 'em you already did it at
         another place earlier. No harm, no
         foul, but ya' get a free drink out of
         it. But maybe a little later in the
         evening...you've had a few drinks...
         you're kinda loosey goosey...you're
         safe with your girls...then some
         kinda cute, kinda hot, kinda sexy,
         hysterically funny, but not funny-
         looking guy comes up and says it.
         Then...maybe you did it earlier...
         maybe you didn't.

They stand up to leave.

                    ARLENE
         I'm gonna have fuckin' guys buggin'
         me all night.

                    JUNGLE JULIA
         Ain't nobody gonna be buggin' ya',
         that's why you got mama here to
         shoo them flies away.

EXT. GÜERO'S—NIGHT

We see POV from the Driver in the muscle car; the
three girls walk out of Güero's. The same bluesy rock
number that was playing as the girls went in is still
playing as they walk out.

One of the girls trips a little bit on the steps going
down, indicating they've polished off a few
margaritas.

We hear the Driver laugh off screen.

                                        FADE TO BLACK:

OVER BLACK

As the song continues...
The TEXT APPEARS:

> "Two Hours later
> at
> Huck's"

FADE UP

EXT. HUCK'S BAR—NIGHT

A different billboard of Jungle Julia, this time
dressed up as a roller derby queen, holding a record
player, and placing the needle on a spinning L.P.
"AUSTIN HOT WAX 505."

Then we see Huck's; it sure as hell's a dive, but in
the words of Julia, "a fucking cool dive." Maybe the
audience notices the girls' white Honda and the
Driver's muscle car in the parking lot, maybe they
don't.

INT. HUCK'S—NIGHT

The song from before continues on Huck's extremely
cool vintage jukebox, the aforementioned Amy.

Jungle Julia, pint of beer in one hand and lit
cigarette in the other, does a very sexy dance to
the bluesey rock classic. For the audience in Huck's
as well as in the movie theatre, she's putting on a
one-ho-show.

Our three-fox posse has collected some stray sniffing
dogs, the aforementioned NATE, OMAR, and DOV.

Dov's talking up Shanna at their beer-spilled,
peanut-shell-strewn table. Omar's drinking Shiner
Bock beer from a pitcher, admiring Julia's dance.
Arlene and Nate are dancing together (he's holding
her from behind and their pelvises are moving
together), which shows Arlene's not a goody two
shoes, she's out to party; she's just not clear about
the new dynamic with her old college pals.

Needless to say, everybody's drunk.

The song ends, and WARREN, the owner-operator of
Huck's, yells to Julia:

                    WARREN
     Now, Julia, if you wanna carry on
     like the main attraction at a
     cathouse with four floors of whores,
     carry on. But if I gotta tell you
     one more goddamn time to put out
     that fucking cigarette, I'm gonna
     treat you just like any other
     belligerent drunk, and climb across
     this bar and hit ya upside the head
     with a horse cock.

Everyone in the place laughs.

Julia rolls her eyes to heaven, blows out a dramatic
stream of smoke (a la Joan Crawford), and bitchy
grinds out her cigarette in the table top (a la Bette
Davis).

                    JUNGLE JULIA
     Happy?

                    WARREN
     As a clam. You may continue your
     one-ho-show.

Nobody's mad at anybody; they're just giving each
other shit.

Julia sits down next to Pete.

                    SHANNA
     When's Lanna-Frank getting here?

                    JUNGLE JULIA
     That's a good fucking question.

She takes out her cell phone and pushes a button,
calling Lanna-Frank.

                    JUNGLE JULIA
                         (pause)
     Where are you?
                         (pause)
     Well come over already, we're
     waiting for you.
                         (pause)
     No, we're not coming over there. You
     come over here like you said you
     would.
                         (pause)
     Chris Simonson is coming.
                         (pause)
     Jessie Letterman too.

                  JUNGLE JULIA
                    (pause)
    Well, not yet, but they're on their
    way. So you get on your way too.
                    (pause)
    Okay, hurry up.

She hangs up the phone, and hits TEXT MESSAGE.

She quickly texts:

    "I can't wait to see you. Hurry!!!!!!"

Goes to the name Chris Simonson and hits send.

    "Your message has been sent."

appears on her screen.

Shanna schools Dov as she drinks a humongous Long
Island iced tea.

                  SHANNA
    Now there's one thing that every girl
    in the whole world whose name is
    Shanna has in common with each other.
    We all hate the name Shauna. And we
    really hate it when people call us
    Shauna.

                  DOV
    So that was a bad move on my part?

                  SHANNA
    Oh yeah. Your fuckability stock is
    plummeting. Just remember, it's
    Shanna Banana, not Shauna Banuna.

Julia's phone rings with a text message. She hits the
menu, and it says a message from: Chris Simonson.

She opens up the electronic mail. It reads:

    "Me too."

She smiles and texts back:

    "XOXO
    J.J."

She hits send.

Omar arrives with shots of Cabo Wabo tequila.

                         OMAR
            Okay, everybody, time for shots.

Everybody groans, but they do them.

We see CUs of all three girls knocking back the
tequila, and making faces, and having an alcohol
tremor.

Arlene stands up, and takes out a pack of cigarettes
called "CAPITOL W LIGHTS."

                        ARLENE
            I'm going out to have a smoke.

Arlene walks outside by herself to the front porch of
Huck's.

EXT. HUCK'S FRONT PORCH—(RAINING) NIGHT

Upon hitting the night air, Arlene immediately sees
it's fuckin' pissin' cats and dogs.

                        ARLENE
            Whoa, when the fuck did this start?

                    FEMALE VOICE (OS)
            About ten minutes ago.

Arlene turns toward the voice. She sees a pretty girl,
late twenties (same age as the other girls), sitting
on a porch swing, smoking a cigarette. Even though
they won't get around to introducing themselves to
each other for a while, this angelic-looking, blonde-
haired, sassy little hippy chick is named PAM.

                         PAM
            Are your windows rolled up?

                        ARLENE
            Yeah.

                         PAM
            Lucky you.

                        ARLENE
            How's it going?

                         PAM
            It could be better.

                        ARLENE
            Havin' a bad night?

                    PAM
          Well, I'm on a date, the highpoint
          of which is me right now, smoking
          this cigarette.

                    ARLENE
          So talking to me is the best part
          of your date?

                    PAM
          Well, you're behind the cigarette
          in popularity, but you're definitely
          way above my date.

Pam was venting and doesn't like how that makes her
sound.

                    PAM
          Awww, he's okay, — he could be okay.

                    ARLENE
          Stuck with a geek.

                    PAM
          NO.—I mean yes, but I don't care
          about that. I'm a big girl, I said
          yes,...but he's just so fucking
          shy, it's starting to creep me out.

                    ARLENE
          Oh, you're stuck with a dateless
          wonder.

                    PAM
          I like the sound of that. What's
          that?

                    ARLENE
          A dateless wonder is a guy who thinks
          about girls a lot but doesn't have
          much social skills. So he doesn't go
          out a lot. But he's not like his
          geeky friends, or his fat friends, or
          his confused sexuality friends, he
          goes out...every once in a while.
          Every once in a while he gets the
          balls to ask a girl out. Now dateless
          wonders usually make it a point to
          ask girls out of their league. Since
          they don't expect to get the date
          anyway, why not aim high.

                         ARLENE
              And every once in a while, they get
              their shit together long enough to be
              charming enough to get a pretty girl
              to say yes. And you're that pretty
              girl.

Pam puts out her cigarette.

                         PAM
              Okay, okay...it's help the
              handicapped week, I guess. Thanks
              to you, I'm ready to go back in
              there and give him another chance
              to get his shit together.

                         ARLENE
              Can you point him out to me?

                         PAM
              He's cute, actually. I mean you
              know, in that way. But no, he's
              genuinely cute.

They open the door to peer in, but when Pam looks
toward her table, new people are sitting at it, and
her date is nowhere to be seen.

                         PAM
              Wait a minute, where the fuck is he?

                         ARLENE
              Wasn't he at your table?

                         PAM
              Yeah, that's what I'm talking
              about, that's where he was supposed
              to be.

                         ARLENE
              Which one is your table?

                         PAM
              The one with the new people sitting
              down is our table.

She looks around in time to see her date's car leaving
the restaurant parking lot.

                         PAM
              Hey, that's my date's car...that's
              my date...
                   (she shouts to him)
              Scott!

She starts walking toward the car, but stops because of the rain.

                    PAM
          Scott!

The car takes off...

...leaving her stranded at the bar.

                    PAM
                 (to herself)
          I don't fucking believe this.
                 (then yelling in
                  frustration)
          I don't fucking believe this!

She yanks out her cell phone and angrily dials Scott.

We lose Arlene at this point, and stay with Pam.

The other end of the cell phone picks up.

                    SCOTT (OS)
          Hello.

                    PAM
          Having fun? Where the fuck you
          think you're going, Scott?

                    SCOTT (OS)
          Look, I didn't think it was going
          well...

                    PAM
          That happens, little boy, and you
          deal with it like a man. You don't
          abandon me like a sniveling little
          fucking worm.

                    SCOTT (OS)
          I didn't think you'd have a
          problem —

                    PAM
          — shut the fuck up and listen. You
          never abandon a woman like that.
          In a fucking bar no less, in the
          fucking rain! You take a woman out,
          safetywise I'm supposed to be in
          your care.

                         PAM
          Or are you such a pathetic little
          fucking soft cock that you didn't
          know that was part of the date
          contract?

                       SCOTT (OS)
          Do you want me to turn around? I
          can still take you home.

                         PAM
          Yeah, I want you to come back here,
          so I can kick your fucking ass in
          front of everybody at this bar,
          that's what I want. I mean it,
          Scott, if I ever see you again, I'm
          gonna kick your fucking ass so bad,
          and you know I can do it too, and I
          don't care who you're with.

                       SCOTT (OS)
          Pam, I'm sorry, I fucked up, I
          know —

                         PAM
          Oh, just write your phone number on
          a gay bar bathroom wall, and fuck
          off.

She hangs up.

She storms back inside the bar.

She goes up to the bartender,

                         PAM
          Can you fucking believe that shit?

                       WARREN
          What?

                         PAM
          Squiddly fuckin' bails on me.

                       WARREN
          You mean you weren't through with
          your date?

                         PAM
          No. I was outside having a smoke
          while he's paying the check and
          sneaking out the fucking back. At
          least I hope he paid the check. Did
          he pay the check?

                    WARREN
          He didn't pay me.

She can't believe it, her cell phone rings.

She lifts it to her ear:

                    PAM
          Hello, Scott.

                    SCOTT (OS)
          Pam, I feel really really bad about
          what I did. Please please please
          let me come back and give you a
          ride home.

                    PAM
          Well I'm sorry you feel "really
          really bad." But let me ask you a
          question. When you were cowardly
          sneaking out the back door, did you
          stop long enough to pay the check
          at least?

There's silence...

Then...

                    SCOTT (OS)
          ...Oh shit...I'm so sorry,
          Pam —

She hangs up the phone.

                    PAM
          Warren, it looks like I owe you
          money.

                    WARREN
          No kidding, how much?

                    PAM
          Not much. We just had a coupla
          beers and some nachos.

                    WARREN
Want me to close you out?

                    PAM
          No, I'll stay. I'll have another
          drink, or two.

                         WARREN
             Well, in that case, how 'bout your
             next drink and the nachos on us.

                          PAM
             That's why I like this place.

                         WARREN
             Membership has its privileges. What
             can I get ya'?

BACK TO ARLENE ON THE PORCH

Arlene's by herself on the porch swing, smoking her
cigarette...

when...

her eyes land on the muscle car from earlier, sitting
in the parking lot.

Her face shows she recognizes the car that seemed
suspicious before.

Something about this car makes her uneasy.

A hand comes up behind her, touching her shoulder and
making her jump.

It's Nate; he laughs at her reaction.

                         ARLENE
             It's not funny, you shitty asshole,
             you scared the fuck outta me! What,
             you think scaring girls is cute?

Nate, palms out, pleading his case.

                          NATE
             I'm sorry, Arlene, I swear I wasn't
             trying to scare you. I just got
             lucky.

                         ARLENE
             Oh, hardy-fuckin'-har.

She tosses her cigarette out in the rain.

                         ARLENE
             Let's go inside.

                        NATE
Wait a minute.

                        ARLENE
What?

                        NATE
I was thinkin' we could make out?

                        ARLENE
What, on the porch swing, not even
in the bar, but in front of the
entrance? Forget it.

                        NATE
No, in my car.

                        ARLENE
              (referring to the rain)
What, out there? It's wet as shit
out there.

                        NATE
Not in my car, it's not.

He takes out an umbrella that opens on cue.

                        NATE
You won't get wet, I promise you.

She gives him a look.

                        ARLENE
You know most guys wouldn't brag
about that.

Nate smiles.

                        NATE
I mean, you won't get rained on.

She still gives him a look.

                        NATE
C'mon, I know you guys are goin' to
Lake LBJ and we can't come.
              (whining)
I wanna make out.

                        ARLENE
Okay, just stop with the whine;
it's not attractive.

She contemplates for a moment...

Nate waits for his fate to be decided...

> ARLENE
> Okay, but I don't want it super
> fucking obvious to everybody in the
> bar we've been gone. So we go in
> your car, and make out for six
> minutes, and that's it. Deal?

> NATE
> Great.

> ARLENE
> No no no no no no, deal or no deal.
> If you're gonna whine when I pull
> the plug at six minutes, we can
> just walk back inside the fucking
> bar right now.

> NATE
> Deal. No whining.

> ARLENE
> And no begging.

> NATE
> No begging, when you say done, it's
> done.

> ARLENE
> I'm gonna remember you said that.
> Okay, let's go.

As she gets under his umbrella, and they walk in the
rain, she says:

> ARLENE
> You got two jobs, to kiss good and
> make sure my hair don't get wet.

BACK IN HUCK'S

Dov and Omar stand up to get more drinks.

> OMAR
> I'm getting more drinks. What can I
> get ya'?

> DOV
> Shanna-Banana?

                         SHANNA
          Another bigass Long Island iced
          tea.

Omar pointing coollike at Julia:

                         OMAR
          Bombay Sapphire and tonic, no ice.

Julia nods her head approvingly.

                      JUNGLE JULIA
          Good boy.

As a new 45 falls on the vintage turntable...and the
needle lowers...

We go behind a Customer sitting at the bar. Using both
hands, he's eating the Huck's Huckin' Nacho Grande
Platter. Which comes with double everything: sour
cream, melted cheese, queso sauce, enchilada sauce,
and chili sauce.

The Customer is not wolfishly devouring it, yet, using
both of his bare hands, he's eating it in a way that
expresses his hearty appetite. And apparently these
nachos are finger-licking good.

Due to the silver satin "Icy Hot" jacket, we can tell
that the Customer and the Driver are the same. But we
can tell more now about him. He appears middle fifties,
but actually might be older. His body is in good, if
well-worn, shape.

In place of a beat-up cowboy hat, he wears a beat-up
pompadour that he keeps afloat with a healthy mixture of
Aqua Net and Tres Flores pomade.

His body language carries that certain breed of redneck
elegance that only rodeo riders and professional stuntmen
have. He listens to the music on the jukebox as he eats
his nachos, and drinks his glass of clear liquid.

We have yet to see him full on, but one more thing we
can tell...

...he has a big scar running down his face.

Dov and Omar show up at the bar next to the
Customer/Driver.

                         DOV
          Two soldiers of Shiner. One bigass
          Long Island iced tea.

> > OMAR
> And one Bombay Sapphire and tonic.

> > WARREN
> Sure you don't want another pitcher
> of Shiner?

> > OMAR
> Nope, we want the soldiers.

> > WARREN
> Three soldiers, comin' up.

INT. NATE'S CAR (PARKED)—RAINING—NIGHT

Arlene and Nate make out as the car radio plays and
the rain splashes against the windows.

As they kiss in the backseat, Arlene raises her ass
off the seat a little bit to slide her shorts off her
crotch and down to her knees.

She takes his hand, as they kiss, and puts it between
her legs.

They kiss longer...

... ...till...

...she breaks the kiss and the mood by saying:

> > ARLENE
> Goddamnit. Do I actually hafta say
> the words "finger fuck me?"

> > NATE
> Oh, I'm sorry —

She irritatedly waves him away.

> > ARLENE
> Forget it.

She slides her pants back up.

Nate's window of opportunity has slammed shut.

CUT BACK TO

INT. HUCK'S—NIGHT

The Customer/Driver eats his nachos near the two young men without either looking or even glancing in their direction.

Dov in pussy pointers mode.

> DOV
> Look, you can't look like you're trying to get her out of here before Christian Simonson shows up. But you gotta get her outta here before Christian Simonson shows up.

> OMAR
> Yeah, but they're going to Shanna's daddy's cabin on Lake LBJ and it's no guys, absolutely no guys.

> DOV
> So after we bring the girls the drinks, in fairly rapid order, but not obvious, we order two more rounds of shots.

> OMAR
> She ain't gonna fall for that.

> DOV
> We'll be very convincing. And now's the time to turn up the volume. No more fuckin' around. We go to Jäger shots.

> OMAR
> Oh man, they're not gonna drink that shit.

> DOV
> Dude, as long as a guy's buyin' the booze, a bitch'll drink anything. Look, we can at least get one Jäger shot down these bitches' throats. After that shot, we'll see if they have another Jäger shot in 'em. You never know. That could be the shot that puts them past the point of fuck-it. But I know I can, at least, get Shanna to do a buttery nipple shot. What's Julia's sweet shot?

                              OMAR
               Key lime pie.

                               DOV
               C'mon, you can get her to do one
               more for dessert.

Arlene and Nate walk back in the bar.

The Customer/Driver looks over his shoulder, at Dov
and Omar handing the Long Island iced tea and the gin
and tonic to the ladies.

                               DOV
               Oh great, I'm just getting more
               drinks. What can I get ya'?

                              NATE
               Another Shiner.

Arlene notices Pam at the bar, drinking a drink out of
a glass cowboy boot.

                             ARLENE
                           (to Pam)
               What's that?

                              PAM
               It's a Cadillac margarita on the
               rocks made with Cabo Wabo tequila.
               Have a sip.

Arlene takes it.

                             ARLENE
               Uuuumm, that's good. (to Pete) I'll
               have this. (to Pam) Would you like
               to join our party?

Pam takes a look over at their table, sees Jungle
Julia, and says:

                              PAM
               No, that's okay. I'll just sit at
               the bar and play the barfly vixen.

Arlene and Nate sit back down at their table.

                          JUNGLE JULIA
               And where did you two disappear to?

                    ARLENE
          I had to get something out of the
          car, and Nate was gentlemanly
          enough to escort me with his
          umbrella.

                    JUNGLE JULIA
          Good for you, Nate.

                    ARLENE
          See that pretty girl by herself at
          the bar?

Julia meows.

                    JUNGLE JULIA
          Who, the dirty hippy?

                    ARLENE
                    (laughs)
          Meow. She's not a hippy.

                    JUNGLE JULIA
          She might as well be a hippy.

                    ARLENE
          Do you know what just happened to her?

                    JUNGLE JULIA
          No, but I know she's a skinny fake
          blonde bitch.

Everybody at the table laughs.

                    JUNGLE JULIA
          Oh, I'm sorry, you were telling a
          story. What about her?

The old pop and crackly 45 continues its revolutions
on the vintage jukebox. The bass-heavy speaker at the
bottom booms.

Referring to the record on the jukebox, the bartender,
Warren, yells out:

                    WARREN
          Stax records, best goddamn label
          ever.
                    (he yells to the
                    girls' table)
          Julia, you play this?

                    JUNGLE JULIA
          You know I did, Warren. I know how
          to take care of my man.

Julia holds up her gin and tonic, and says:

                    JUNGLE JULIA
          Here's to Warren's jukebox.

Everybody at the table raises their glass.

                         DOV
          You know what, we should do a shot
          of Jäger in honor of Warren's
          jukebox.

Julia and the girls are responding negatively to Dov's
idea.

                    JUNGLE JULIA
          Uh-huh, I ain't drinkin' no goddamn
          Jäger shot.

                         DOV
          Why not?

                    JUNGLE JULIA
          Because I don't wanna fuck any of
          y'all, that's why.

The girls laugh.

She puts her hand on Omar's shoulder.

                    JUNGLE JULIA
          Not tonight anyway.

Arlene, glass cowboy boot in hand, turns and catches
eyes with Pam, glass cowboy boot in hand.

They smile and silently cheer each other across the
room.

Pam turns away, to Warren, the bartender.

                         PAM
          So, Warren, is there anyone here at
          the bar you'd vouch for to give me
          a ride home?

The key to the muscle car with the spark plug attached
is tossed onto the bar in front of her with a loud thud.

She looks up and sees the Driver seated one seat away.

We see him clearly now, no more obscure bullshit.
He has a big scar on his face from what looks like a
previous accident. But the scar doesn't make him look
grotesque. It makes him look kinda cool.

                    DRIVER
Fair lady, your chariot awaits.

                    PAM
You've been eavesdropping on me?

                    DRIVER
Well, there's eavesdropping and
can't help but hear. I think I
belong in the later category.

                    PAM
You offering me a ride home, Icy
Hot?

                    ICY HOT
I'm offering you a lift, if when I'm
ready to leave, you are too.

                    PAM
When are you thinking about
leaving?

                    ICY HOT
Truthfully, I'm not thinking about
it. But when I do, you'll be the
first to know.

                    PAM
Will you be able to drive later?

                    ICY HOT
I know looks can be deceiving, but
I'm a teetotaler. I've been drinking
club soda and lime all night. I'm
building up to my big drink.

                    PAM
What's that?

                    ICY HOT
Virgin Piña Colada.

                    PAM
Why would a person who doesn't drink
spend hours in a bar
drinking water?

                     ICY HOT
        You know, a bar offers all kinds of
        things other than alcohol?

                     PAM
        Like what?

                     ICY HOT
        Women.

Icy Hot flirting, but not putting the bite on Pam; he's
just being flirtatiously intriguing.

                     ICY HOT
        Nacho Grande Platters. The
        fellowship of some fascinating
        individuals, like Warren here.

She laughs.

                     ICY HOT
        The alcohol is just a lubricant for
        the individual encounters that a
        barroom offers.

                     PAM
        Is that cowboy wisdom?

                     ICY HOT
        I'm not a cowboy, I'm a stuntman.
        Very easy mistake to make, Pam.

                     PAM
        How do you know my name?

                     ICY HOT
        When you were talking to Warren, I
        couldn't help but hear.

                     PAM
        Fair enough. What's your name, Icy?

                     ICY HOT
        Stuntman Mike.

                     PAM
        Stuntman Mike's your name?

                 STUNTMAN MIKE
        Ask anybody.

Pam turns to Warren.

                    PAM
          Hey, Warren, who is this guy?

                  WARREN
          That's Stuntman Mike.

                    PAM
          And who the hell's Stuntman Mike?

                  WARREN
          He's a stuntman.

                    PAM
          If he gives me a lift home later,
          would you vouch for him?

                  WARREN
          All I can say is he's never raped
          me. And it's not like I haven't
          worn provocative clothing in front
          of him either.

Our girls' table shouts for Warren:

                JUNGLE JULIA
          Warren, six shots of Wild Turkey.
                  (to the guys)
          If we're doing shots, we're gonna
          do Junior Bonner style grown folk
          shots. No college kid Slurpee
          shots. And if you want to do a shot
          after this, we do Early Time. Got
          it?

                   PETE
          Got it.

                JUNGLE JULIA
                (with a smile)
          Now go fetch me my Turkey.

Six shots of Wild Turkey shots are poured by Warren on
the bar. Stuntman Mike notices it and Dov and Arlene
coming to the bar to pick up the shots.

Arlene comes up to Pam.

                  ARLENE
          We're all doing Wild Turkey shots;
          do one with us?

Pam looks over at the table and sees Julia and Shanna.

                              PAM
                    What's your name, honey?

                              ARLENE
                    Arlene.

                              PAM
                    Hi, Arlene. I'm Pam.

                              ARLENE
                    What's up, Pam.

                              PAM
                    Now look, you're very sweet, and
                    you're totally cool...

As Pam tells her this, Arlene notices Stuntman Mike,
on the barstool next to Pam. She instantly knows he's
the Driver of the muscle car from before and the one
parked right outside.

He smiles at Arlene.

A chill runs through her.

                              PAM
                    Arlene, party of one.

Arlene realizes she just spaced out.

                              ARLENE
                    Oh, I'm sorry, I just spaced. What
                    did you say?

                              PAM
                    I said: me and your friends aren't
                    exactly B.F.F. As a matter of fact,
                    I hate your fuckin' friends. No
                    offense to you, angel.

                              ARLENE
                    Oh, that's okay, none taken. Maybe
                    I'll see you around.

Arlene carries the shots back to her table. Everybody
takes them.

After Arlene does her Wild Turkey shot, her eyes come
up on Stuntman Mike by the bar. He's looking right at
her, watching her do her whiskey shot. He turns
casually and continues talking to Pam.

This character makes Arlene feel more and more uneasy.

BACK TO PAM

> PAM
> Well, Stuntman Mike, since I have a
> tab here, can I buy you that Virgin
> Piña Colada?

> STUNTMAN MIKE
> Well, thank you, Pam, that would be
> lovely.

> PAM
> Warren, a Virgin Piña Colada for my
> stuntman friend, and I'll have
> another Cadillac Cabo Wabo
> margarita.

> WARREN
> Cabo Wabo margarita.

INSERT

A finger punches a button with the symbol of a phone on
it.

CELL PHONE SCREEN

It says:

> "dialing
> Chris Simonson"

> JUNGLE JULIA
> (into phone)
> Get your ass over here. We're
> fuckin' bored.
> (pause)
> C'mon, I'm missing you. You're
> making me wait and it's mean.
> (pause)
> Well then, prove it.
> (pause)
> Dial me when you're on your way.

BACK TO PAM

> STUNTMAN MIKE
> So, Pam, what do you do?

> PAM
> That's a very good question,
> Stuntman Mike. At this moment,
> unfortunately, not a fuckin' thing.

Their drinks arrive. Stuntman Mike takes a sip of the tall, foamy, white cocktail.

> STUNTMAN MIKE
> Well, let me put it this way, when last it was you did something, what did you do?

> PAM
> The last job I had, I was a personal assistant.

> STUNTMAN MIKE
> Really? Whose personal assistant?

> PAM
> Do you know who Jessie Letterman is?

> STUNTMAN MIKE
> The Austin director who did "Potheads"?

> PAM
> Yeah, well, I worked over at his company Roadblock for a little while, then I became his personal assistant for a couple years, then we started making out, then we had a little thing, and then it was best to leave.

> STUNTMAN MIKE
> He couldn't afford to have your ass around, huh?

> PAM
> No, it wasn't that. You just can't get coffee for a guy whose dick you're suckin'. It's one of those things that can't help but rub you the wrong way.

> STUNTMAN MIKE
> Is that the kind of job you want next?

> PAM
> What, suckin' dick?

> STUNTMAN MIKE
> No, personal assistant.

                    PAM
Well, that's the million dollar
question I've got less than five
weeks to decide.

                STUNTMAN MIKE
Well, it's funny you should bring
that up, because you know, I was
thinking about hiring a personal
assistant.

                    PAM
                (laughing)
No kidding.

                STUNTMAN MIKE
Yeah, I think it could really help
relieve stress in my life, if I had
an assistant helping me cope.

                    PAM
            (with a smile on her face)
Well, what kind of things would you
need a personal assistant to do?

                STUNTMAN MIKE
Oh, I don't know, you know more
about how this stuff works. What do
you think you should do for me?

                    PAM
That's not the way it works.

                STUNTMAN MIKE
Okay, what did you do for Jessie?

                    PAM
Well, if he was shooting I would
wake him up, and have a cup of
coffee ready —

                STUNTMAN MIKE
You did that?

                    PAM
Yeah.

                STUNTMAN MIKE
                (laughing)
Baby, you're hired.

JUNGLE JULIA AND CO

We cut back to them as Shanna is in mid story...

                    SHANNA
          — I come over to her apartment at
          2:30 in the afternoon. She's layin'
          on the couch like a house cat.

                    ARLENE
          Naturally —

                    SHANNA
          Watchin' Sponge Bob Square Pants on
          HD T.V., blarin' it so loud, you'd
          think she was listin' to Pink
          fuckin' Floyd, takin' a big ass
          bong hit, and eatin' a Jumbo Jack.

                    JUNGLE JULIA
          Hey, that's a discombobulated day
          in the life of a drive time DJ. I
          get off work at 10:00am, I'm at
          home by 10:30. By 11:00 I'm
          snuggled up on my comfy couch, in
          my pajamas, hittin' the bong. I
          watch "I Love Lucy" at eleven
          O'clock. "The Andy Griffith Show" —
          which my dad use to always say; Don
          Knotts was the funniest White Man
          who ever lived. I watch that at
          eleven-thirty. At 12:00, I watch
          back to back episodes of "The Fresh
          Prince of Bel Air." At 1:00 I watch
          back to back episodes of "Moesha."
          At 2:00 I watch Sponge Bob Square
          Pants. At 2:30 I watch "Pinky and
          the Brain." At 3:00 I watch back to
          back episodes of "Sister Sister."
          And at 4:00 I watch "Tyra." Then I
          eat a big bowl of cereal, get
          unstoned and go about my day.

                    NATE
          What do you mean get unstoned?

Like a doctor;

                    JUNGLE JULIA
          Dairy fucks up your high. You wanna
          get unhigh fast, eat a bowl of
          cereal.

Looking like she was caught out in the rain, white trash pot dealer LANNA-FRANK, followed by two other BADASS-LOOKING GIRLS (no college kids these), walk through the door.

Julia, Shanna, and the guys greet them with a big cheer.

Lanna-Frank walks over to the bar to give Warren some love.

She even knows Pam, and kisses her, then heads to Julia's table.

>   STUNTMAN MIKE
>   This Lanna-Frank would seem to be
>   quite a popular young lady.

>   PAM
>   (meow)
>   When your drug dealer finally
>   arrives, you're usually very happy
>   to see them.

Stuntman Mike looks over in the table's direction and sees Lanna-Frank and her friends being introduced to Arlene and joining the table.

She takes a bag of weed out of her pocket and shows it to the table. Stuntman Mike clocks all of this.

Pam says to Stuntman Mike, looking over at Julia's table:

>   PAM
>   Take a picture, it lasts longer.

>   STUNTMAN MIKE
>   What?

>   PAM
>   That table seems to keep getting
>   your attention.

>   STUNTMAN MIKE
>   Is that jealousy I detect, little
>   one?

>   PAM
>   Hardly. But if you want to hook up
>   with Jungle Julia, there's an easy
>   way to do that.

>   STUNTMAN MIKE
>   Really, and what would that be?

                              PAM
               Get famous. Then you won't have to
               find her, she'll find you. You don't
               even want to know what she did for
               that billboard.

She raises her glass to toast J.J.:

                              PAM
               Enjoy it, cocksucker, you've earned
               it.

                        STUNTMAN MIKE
               What did she ever do to you?

                              PAM
               We went through school together, from
               kindergarten through high school,
               that's what she did. She was her
               height right now at twelve. She was a
               monster. Half the guys she still
               fucks from the old class, she used to
               beat up and terrorize them in the
               fifth grade.

                        STUNTMAN MIKE
               I see. She used to beat you up and
               take your chocolate milk, huh?

                              PAM
               That pituitary case might of kicked
               my ass a couple of times — sorry,
               I'm built like a girl, not a black
               man — but I would die before I ever
               gave Julia Lucai my chocolate milk.
               I've kissed a lot of ass in my day,
               but I'll be damned I kiss that
               bitch's ass.

JUNGLE JULIA AND ARLENE

                           ARLENE
               So Julia, have you booked all the
               bands for SXSW yet?

                        JUNGLE JULIA
               Here it comes.

                           ARLENE
               What?

                        JUNGLE JULIA
               It's nothing personal, honey, it's
               just everybody knows a band.

                    JUNGLE JULIA
And every band wants to play SXSW.
And everybody thinks it's as easy
as pie for me

                    ARLENE
Look, I'm sorry

                    JUNGLE JULIA
— I get crabby, but the truth is
I've found some good bands that
way. What's their name?

                    ARLENE
What?

                    JUNGLE JULIA
The band you like, what's their
name?

                    ARLENE
I didn't say I like them.

                    JUNGLE JULIA
You don't like them?

                    ARLENE
I've never heard them. It's a
friend from work's band. I mean I
have their CD; it's been sitting on
my kitchen counter for months, but
I haven't listened to it yet.

                    JUNGLE JULIA
But you want me to?

                    ARLENE
Would you?

                    JUNGLE JULIA
Sure. What's the name of the group?

                    ARLENE
The Idols.

                    JUNGLE JULIA
The Eyeballs?

                    ARLENE
The Idols.

                    LANNA-FRANK
Who's coming outside to smoke out?

All three of the guys stand up.

                    JUNGLE JULIA
          Look, we can't all go out there in
          mass exodus. Omar, you stay and
          watch the table.

Omar is crestfallen.

                    ARLENE
          No, that's okay, I'll stay.
                    (to Shanna)
          Can I speak with you for a minute?

                    SHANNA
          Sure, honey.
                    (to the others)
          I'll see y'all out there.

Julia, Lanna-Frank, her friends, and the boys head for
the door.

INSERT

The lever of a cigarette machine is pulled out.

A pack of Red Apple cigarettes falls to the machine's
catchall.

Julia takes it and leads her little entourage to the
porch when a female BAR PATRON approaches her.

                    BAR PATRON
          Excuse me, are you Jungle Julia
          Lucai?

                    JUNGLE JULIA
          Yes, I am.

                    BAR PATRON
          You know I was listening to your
          show once and you were talking
          about —

                    JUNGLE JULIA
          I'm sure I don't remember. What's
          your name?

                    BAR PATRON
          Peg.

                    JUNGLE JULIA
          Well, Peg, my friends and I are
          going out for a smoke.

Peg holds up a silver digital camera.

                    PEG
          I hate to ask you —

                    JUNGLE JULIA
          — no you don't.

                    PEG
          — I'm sorry?

                    JUNGLE JULIA
          You want me to take a picture with
          you — fine — but don't tell me how
          you hate asking me.

                    PEG
          Can I take a picture?

                    JUNGLE JULIA
          Sure.

                    PEG
                 (to Lanna-Frank)
          Would you take it?

Peg and Julia pose smiling, while Lanna-Frank fumbles
around with the digital camera.

                    JUNGLE JULIA
          I hate these fuckin' digital pieces
          of shit cameras nobody knows how to
          use. Those disposable film cameras
          were the bomb. Pitch the digital
          shit and get a real camera.

Lanna-Frank takes the photo.

EXT. HUCK'S PORCH (RAIN)—NIGHT

The rain comes down pissing.

INSERT

Oil imbedded in the highway is being brought up by the
rain.

Stuntman Mike, now outside having a smoke, watches the
rain, and the wet highway, as he smokes his
Chesterfield.

You can tell he's really enjoying the rain.

Julia and Lanna-Frank sit on the porch swing. The guys
hover around them, sharing the joint.

Stuntman Mike turns in her direction.

>   STUNTMAN MIKE
>   Are you famous or something?

>   JUNGLE JULIA
>   Or something.

>   STUNTMAN MIKE
>   No, really, what do you do?

>   JUNGLE JULIA
>   Really? What I do is work my ass
>   off to get my own record label off
>   the ground. But why that girl
>   wanted a picture of me is because
>   I'm a local D.J.

Stuntman Mike gets up and moves toward the pot-smoking crowd.

>   STUNTMAN MIKE
>   Wait a minute, you got a billboard
>   by Big Kahuna Burger, don'tcha?

Julia turns to Lanna-Frank.

>   JUNGLE JULIA
>   See, I told you, I'm not really
>   that famous, I'm just that
>   recognizable. If you know what I
>   look like, you'll know me when you
>   see me.
>   (holding out her hand)
>   Jungle Julia Lucai.

>   STUNTMAN MIKE
>   Stuntman Mike Mikki.

>   JUNGLE JULIA
>   Well, it's good to meet you,
>   Stuntman Mike. Now my friends and I
>   are going to continue to get our
>   weed on. Would you care for some?

>   STUNTMAN MIKE
>   Thank you, Julia, but just the
>   same, no thanks.

>   JUNGLE JULIA
>   Suit yourself.

INT. GIRLS BATHROOM—NIGHT

Arlene and Shanna talk in the ladies room.

> ARLENE
> She just made me feel like an idiot
> for asking her about her stupid
> SXSW.

> SHANNA
> It's just that time of year where
> that's all anybody asks her about.

> ARLENE
> That's all she ever talks about.
> But that doesn't mean she's gotta
> be a shitty ass about it...look I'm
> here for four days, I'm just
> getting a little sick of the Jungle
> Julia show.

> SHANNA
> Look, Julia's always given herself
> complete permission to be a bitch;
> it's one of the cool things about
> her. And now she's a star —

> ARLENE
> Nigga please, she's not a star! At
> the most, you could consider her a
> local celebrity. Fuckin' Superhead
> is more famous than her. And what's
> this bullshit about Chris Simonson
> putting her in a movie? Am I the
> only one who remember how bad she
> sucked in that play?

> SHANNA
> Hey, that took balls.

> ARLENE
> In a cast of amateurs she
> distinguished herself as being the
> lousiest.

They both bust out laughing and say in unison:

> ARLENE/SHANNA
> Thank you, Grace.

Obviously a private joke only they get.

                              SHANNA
                    Give her a break; not everybody was
                    born to play Ibsen.

                              ARLENE
                    Least of all that bitch.

They laugh again.

                              ARLENE
                    Don't worry, I'm not really mad-
                    mad. I'm just havin' a little Julia
                    detest fest to get the
                    irritatedness out of my system.

BACK ON THE PORCH

Julia takes a hit on the porch swing, her long legs
out in front of her, her bare feet up on the wood
porchrail; the rain is splashing on them.

Stuntman Mike stands up and heads over to them again.

Julia says to the group.

                         JUNGLE JULIA
                    Uh-oh, don't look now but
                    Cannonball Run's coming over.

                         STUNTMAN MIKE
                    You know, there's a T. S. Eliot
                    poem about rain just like tonight.

                         JUNGLE JULIA
                    We're high Mike, spare us the T. S.
                    Fuckin' Eliot.

Lanna-Frank laughs.

                         STUNTMAN MIKE
                    Okay, no poetry and I'm going back
                    inside, but before I go, there is
                    one thing I'm afraid I must point
                    out. Your feet are going to get
                    wet.

                         JUNGLE JULIA
                    I haven't given you permission to
                    concern yourself with my feet.

Lanna-Frank and her friends laugh.

Stuntman Mike gets cold. Looks at them, then to Julia.

> STUNTMAN MIKE
> Come again?

> JUNGLE JULIA
> You told me my feet were getting
> wet. Yes, they are. Now I'm telling
> you, don't worry about it.

Stuntman Mike gets a little scary, and just dead
stares at her.

She comes back the same.

> JUNGLE JULIA
> — I mean it. Don't worry about my
> feet. I don't even want you to
> think about them.

He looks at her.

> JUNGLE JULIA
> I said, stop thinking about them.

A moment passes between the two.

Then Stuntman Mike turns back into the flirtatious old
fool.

> STUNTMAN MIKE
> Well, we could fight about this. But
> as a rule, I usually pay women to
> beat the crap outta me.

This makes Julia laugh.

> JUNGLE JULIA
> Yeah, you wish.

She holds out her hand.

> JUNGLE JULIA
> You may kiss it.

> STUNTMAN MIKE
> Why, of course, my dear lady...

> JUNGLE JULIA
> That doesn't mean a soliloquy, just
> kiss it.

He kisses it, till she yanks it away.

                    JUNGLE JULIA
          That's enough; now be gone.

                  STUNTMAN MIKE
          As you wish, my fair lady.

BACK IN THE BAR

Pam's bullshitting with Warren. Stuntman Mike rejoins
them.

                        PAM
                (referring to Warren)
          You got some voucher here. I asked
          him what movies you worked on, no
          fucking clue.

                      WARREN
          Well, technically, I don't know
          he's ever done anything for sure.
          He shows me an old episode of "High
          Chaparral," a guy falls off a
          horse, he says it's him...okay
          ...could be.

                    STUNTMAN MIKE
          Do you know the show "The
          Virginian"?

Pam shakes her head no.

                    STUNTMAN MIKE
          There was a actor on that show,
          Gary Clarke, I kinda looked like
          him a bit. Obviously before I cut —
          (referring to the scar on his face)
          — myself shaving.

                        PAM
          I like it.

                    STUNTMAN MIKE
          Well, damn, if you ain't so sweet
          you make sugar taste just like
          salt. Well, anyway, I did a lot of
          Virginian's doubling for Gary
          Clarke, then that show turned into
          "The Men of Shilo" and they brought
          Lee Majors on, and I doubled him.

                    STUNTMAN MIKE
          Then from that point on, I mostly
          specialized in car stunts. I worked
          almost the whole third season of
          "Vegas." I was Robert Urich's
          driving double. Bob did another
          show, "Gavilan," he brought me on
          to that one. Till...
                    (he refocuses on Pam)
          Do you know any of these shows or
          people I'm talkin' about?

She apologetically shakes her head no.

                    PAM
          Sorry.

Warren approaches.

                    WARREN
          I hate to tell you this, Mike, but
          dropping Gary Clarke's name don't
          get Gary Clarke pussy no more.

Stuntman Mike and Pam laugh.

                    STUNTMAN MIKE
          No, I suppose it don't.

                    PAM
          So how exactly does one become a
          stuntman?

                    STUNTMAN MIKE
          Well, in Hollywood anybody fool
          enough to throw themselves down a
          flight of stairs can usually find
          somebody to pay ya' fer it. But
          really, I got into the business the
          way most people get in the stunt
          business.

                    PAM
          And how's that?

                    STUNTMAN MIKE
          My brother got me in it.

                    PAM
          Who's your brother?

                    STUNTMAN MIKE
          Stuntman Bob.

                    PAM
          Ask a stupid question, get a stupid
          answer.

Stuntman Mike notices Arlene and Shanna walk out to
the porch.

                STUNTMAN MIKE
          I tell ya', Pam, I think it's gettin'
          to be about that time. But why don't I
          order you one more boot, and I'll go
          out on the porch and have one more
          smoke.

                    PAM
          Sounds good to me.

He smiles and slides off the barstool.

                STUNTMAN MIKE
          Hey, Warren, I think my little
          hippy friend here's thirsty.

BACK ON THE PORCH

The rain suddenly stops; they all notice it except
Julia, who's busy texting on her cell phone.

INSERT: TEXT MESSAGE SCREEN

                    "Your a asshole."
Then...

                "Your message has been sent."

Julia and Omar sit on the porch swing, surrounded by
their posse, passing a joint.

Lanna-Frank leans close to Julia and whispers in her
ear:

                LANNA-FRANK
          Can my friends come up to the lake?

Julia says, louder than she needs to:

                JUNGLE JULIA
          I didn't invite them bitches.

                LANNA-FRANK
          Well, I kinda tole 'em —

                JUNGLE JULIA
          — well, then you just untell them.

Arlene and Shanna walk out on the porch.

Julia slaps Omar on the arm and says:

> JUNGLE JULIA
> Get up and offer the lady your
> seat.

Pete stands up.

> JUNGLE JULIA
> Come here, baby.

Arlene sits next to Julia on the porch swing and hugs
her waist, putting her head on J.J.'s shoulder. Jungle
Julia wraps her long arm around her, talking low to
Arlene like a lover.

> JUNGLE JULIA
> How's my girl holding up?

> ARLENE
> (in a pouty voice)
> I'm okay. But you were mean to me.

> JUNGLE JULIA
> I wasn't mean, I was rude; there's
> a difference. Anywho, I'm sorry. Do
> you forgive me?

Arlene exaggeratedly nods her head yes.

> ARLENE
> But you hafta be real nice to me
> for the whole rest of the time I'm
> here.

> JUNGLE JULIA
> Promise.
> (pause)
> Are you ready to go to the lake?

She nods her head yes.

> JUNGLE JULIA
> How 'bout your little friend; you
> want to bring him?

> ARLENE
> I thought no boys?

                    JUNGLE JULIA
          If you really want him to come,
          Shanna won't mind. So how 'bout it,
          boys or just us girls?

Arlene squeezes Julia tighter.

                    ARLENE
          Us girls.

                    JUNGLE JULIA
          Good idea.

Then two beers come into FRAME.

                    VOICE (OS)
          Ladies.

Both Julia and Arlene take the beers without looking up.

We in the audience notice the hand offering the beers
wears a black leather glove.

                    VOICE (OS)
          Cheers, Butterfly.

They look up to cheers and see:

Stuntman Mike, sitting on his haunches.

                    STUNTMAN MIKE
          "The woods are lovely
          dark and deep
          And I have promises to keep
          And miles to go before I sleep."
          Did you hear me, Butterfly, miles to
          go before you sleep.

                    JUNGLE JULIA
          Sorry, Stuntman Burt —

                    STUNTMAN MIKE
          — Stuntman Mike.

                    JUNGLE JULIA
          — Mike, she already broke off that
          dance.

Stuntman Mike looks at Arlene; she's still a little
frightened of him.

But for whatever reason, he's not as scary now. In fact,
there's something rather intimate about his manner that
actually has a strange effect on the drunk Arlene.

> STUNTMAN MIKE
> Is that true? Did I miss my chance?

She doesn't want to give him a lap dance; she's still
creeped by him, but for whatever reason, she can't
bring herself to lie to him. So she doesn't answer at
all. She just looks back at him, fragilely.

> STUNTMAN MIKE
> Do I frighten you?

She nods her head yes.

> STUNTMAN MIKE
> Is it my scar?

She shakes her head no.

> ARLENE
> It's your car.

Stuntman Mike smiles apologetically.

> STUNTMAN MIKE
> Yeah, I know. Sorry, it's my mom's
> car.

This makes Arlene smile.

> ARLENE
> Have you been following us?

> STUNTMAN MIKE
> Nope. But that's what I like about
> Austin. It's so damn small.

> JUNGLE JULIA
> You've seen this guy before?

> ARLENE
> I saw him outside of Güero's.

> STUNTMAN MIKE
> I saw you outside of Güero's too.
> You saw my car, I saw your legs. I
> ain't stalkin' y'all, but I didn't
> say I wasn't a wolf.

> ARLENE
> So you really weren't following us?

                    STUNTMAN MIKE
          I wasn't following you, Butterfly, I
          just got lucky.

This makes the pretty drunk girl smile.

                    STUNTMAN MIKE
          So how 'bout that lap dance?

                    JUNGLE JULIA
          Sorry, it was a one time only
          offer, and she did it at Antoine's
          earlier this evening.

                    STUNTMAN MIKE
          No, she didn't.

                    ARLENE
          How do you know?

                    STUNTMAN MIKE
          I'm good that way. You look a
          little touchéd.

                    ARLENE
          What's touchéd?

                    STUNTMAN MIKE
          Wounded, slightly.

                    ARLENE
          Why should I be wounded?

                    STUNTMAN MIKE
          Because you expected guys to be
          pestering you all night. But from
          your look I can tell nobody
          pestered you at all. It kinda hurt
          your feelings a little bit, didn't
          it? There are few things as
          fetching as a bruised ego on a
          beautiful angel.
                    (pause)
          So how 'bout that lap dance?

                    ARLENE
          I think I'm gonna have to give you
          a rain check.

                    STUNTMAN MIKE
          Well, since you're leavin' in the
          next couple of days, that rain
          check'll be worthless.

            STUNTMAN MIKE
But that's okay. I understand if I
make you uncomfortable. You're still
a nice girl. I still like you.
However, I must warn you of
somethin'. You know how people say:
"You're okay in my book." Or "In my
book that's no good." Well, I
actually have a book.

He takes out a small little red book.

            STUNTMAN MIKE
And everybody I ever meet goes in
this book. And now I've met you,
you're going in the book. And I'm
goin' to write only nice things,
except I will be forced to file you
under chicken shit.

            ARLENE
And what if I did it?

He gets real quiet.

            STUNTMAN MIKE
Well, I definitely couldn't file you
under chicken shit then, now could
I?

            ARLENE
What's your name?

            STUNTMAN MIKE
Stuntman Mike.

            ARLENE
Well, Stuntman Mike, I'm Butterfly.
My friend Jungle Julia over here
tells me that jukebox inside is
pretty impressive.

            STUNTMAN MIKE
It is.

            ARLENE
Pick out a good song for your lap
dance.

He smiles.

            ARLENE
Mike?

                         STUNTMAN MIKE
          Yeah?

                           ARLENE
          No touch.

                         STUNTMAN MIKE
          I know.

                           ARLENE
          I touch you. You don't touch me.

He nods his head yes.

BACK INSIDE

Stuntman Mike puts a quarter in the jukebox.

A cool fifties oldie comes from the vintage jukebox.

He takes a chair and puts it in the middle of the
room...

...then sits down on it.

Arlene struts up to him and, as all eyes are on them,
performs a smokin' lap dance.

Her girls, and the bar, with the possible exception of
Nate, cheer her on.

Pam and Warren can't wipe the smiles off of their faces.

By the end, Jungle Julia is taking photos with her
instamatic, as Arlene and Mike do funny sexy poses.

Before the song ends, Arlene finishes up; she doesn't
give Mike a kiss, but very lovingly holds his face in
her two hands, like the sweet Italian mama that she
is.

And as the song concludes, without another word, the
girls dance out the door of the bar and leave.

Leaving Stuntman Mike smiling, sitting on his chair.

When he stands, Warren and Pam applaud him.

                           WARREN
          You know, maybe it was you who fell
          off that horse.

                            PAM
          You ready to go, Fonzie?

                    STUNTMAN MIKE
I do believe it's about that time.

EXT. HUCK'S—NIGHT

Stuntman Mike leads Pam out of the bar, toward his car.

In the b.g., the girls are arguing about who's sober
enough to drive, leaving their male admirers whining
to go with them.

                    JUNGLE JULIA
         Yeah, keep it up, nothing makes me
         wanna fuck more then men whining.

Lanna-Frank wins the I'm the least drunk argument—the
most stoned, but least drunk. So she gets behind the
wheel, and the other girls, Julia, Arlene, and Shanna,
pile in.

But that's in the b.g. We stay with Stuntman Mike and
Pam.

He leads her up to his wicked automobile.

Pam is taken by the sight of the badass black muscle car.

                    PAM
         Wow. That's fuckin' scary.

                    STUNTMAN MIKE
         Well, I wanted it to be impressive,
         and scary tends to impress.

                    PAM
         Is it safe?

                    STUNTMAN MIKE
         It's better 'en safe. It's Death
         Proof.

                    PAM
         How do you make a car death proof?

                    STUNTMAN MIKE
         That's what stuntmen do. You've seen
         a movie where a car gets into some
         smashup that there ain't no way in
         hell anybody's walkin' away from?

                    PAM
         Yeah.

                    STUNTMAN MIKE
          How do you think they accomplish
          that?

                         PAM
          CGI?

                    STUNTMAN MIKE
          Well, unfortunately, nowadays, more
          often than not, you're right. But
          back in the all or nothin' days,
          the "Vanishing Point" days, the
          "Dirty Mary Crazy Larry" days, they
          were real cars crashin' into real
          cars, with real dumb, real people
          drivin' 'em. So you give the stunt
          team the car you want to smash up,
          they take 'er, reinforce that
          fucker everywhere, and Wa-La. You
          got yourself a death-proof
          automobile.

                         PAM
          That makes sense. I just didn't
          know you could make a car death
          proof.

                    STUNTMAN MIKE
          I could drive this baby into a
          brick wall at a hundred and twenty-
          five miles a hour, just for the
          experience.

                         PAM
          I'm impressed.

     She peers into the car and sees that the entire
     passenger side is enclosed in Plexiglas.

                         PAM
          Why is the passenger seat in a box?

                    STUNTMAN MIKE
          Well, this is a movie car. And
          sometimes when you're shootin' a
          crash, the director wants a camera
          in the car, shootin' the crash from
          the inside. That's where you put
          the camera. They call it a crash
          box.

He opens the door to the Plexiglas box, offering Pam
to climb in.

>   STUNTMAN MIKE
>   Don't worry, Pam, you'd hafta choke
>   to death on a ham sandwich to die
>   behind the wheel of this baby.

Pam climbs in.

Stuntman Mike shuts the door.

As he walks around to the passenger side, he watches
the other girls peel out, showering gravel. They make
a left onto the highway and disappear.

He smiles after them as he climbs behind the wheel of
his death-proof vehicle.

INT. DEATH PROOF—NIGHT

Stuntman Mike is in the driver's seat.

Pam is in the Plexiglas box.

A Plexiglas wall, with some holes to talk through,
separates them.

Mike has a few different seat belts to snap in place
for himself.

Pam doesn't even have a car seat. She has a post that
sticks out of the floor, that you would attach a camera
to, that she has to balance herself on.

>   PAM
>   You know, when you asked to drive
>   me home, you didn't mention your
>   car didn't have a passenger seat.

>   STUNTMAN MIKE
>   Actually, I didn't ask to drive you
>   home. You asked for a ride, and I
>   said yes. Look at the bright side:
>   I won't be gettin' fresh, puttin'
>   my hand on your knee.

Pam smiles.

                              PAM
                 That is a bright side.

Stuntman Mike smiles back through the Plexiglas.

                        STUNTMAN MIKE
                 I thought so.

He yanks a homemade metal lever that slides a metal
bar into place, locking both doors.

Then starts up his powerful machine.

Pam smiles at the excitement of this trembling
machine.

He slides the car into first and pulls up to the
highway.

                        STUNTMAN MIKE
            Which way you goin', left or right?

                              PAM
                 Right.

                        STUNTMAN MIKE
                 Oh, that's too bad.

Thriller music sting happens on soundtrack.

Still smiling.

                              PAM
                 Why is that too bad?

                        STUNTMAN MIKE
                 Because it was a fifty-fifty shot on
                 whether you'd be goin' left or
                 right. You see we're both goin'
                 left, and you could of just as
                 easily been goin' left too, and if
                 that was the case, then it would of
                 been a while before you would of
                 started getting scared. But since
                 you're goin' the other way, I'm
                 afraid you're gonna hafta get
                 scared immediately.

Pam's smile fades away, as a look of Oh Shit terror
replaces it.

As the look of panic appears...

Stuntman Mike jerks a hard left onto the road.

She's maybe scared shitless, yet Pam is one tough
chick, and she lets lose with a violent stream of
curses aimed at Stuntman Mike.

He shuts her up by turning up the radio real loud and
driving real crazy, tossing her helplessly around the
Plexiglas box, crashing like a rag doll from wall to
wall.

He does things like drive straight toward telephone
poles at full speed, then narrowly miss them.

                    STUNTMAN MIKE
          'Member when I said this car was
          death proof? Well, that wasn't a
          lie. This car is 100 percent death
          proof. Only, to get the benefit of
          it, you really hafta be sitting in
          my seat.

He slams on the brakes and Pam goes flying face first
into the unpaved dashboard. Her face might as well
have exploded.

Stuntman Mike busts a gut laughing.

                    STUNTMAN MIKE
          Boy, ya gotta love them unpaved
          dashboards. Ya get into a wreck, ya
          just hose it off, and sell it to
          somebody else.

Pam's nose is smashed across her face, her front teeth
are knocked out, and her jaw is busted.

But she's still conscious.

                    STUNTMAN MIKE
          Now I gotta catch me my other
          girlfriends.

He speeds down the road.

                                        CUT TO:

INT. SHANNA'S CAR (MOVING)—NIGHT

Lanna-Frank is driving. Julia sits in the passenger
side front seat stretched out with her bare feet up on
the dashboard and pressed into the windshield.

Shanna and Arlene sit in the back.

Julia's on the phone.

> JUNGLE JULIA
> (into phone)
> Thanks, honey,
> > (pause)
> You'll play it next song, right?
> > (pause)
> Good boy.
> > (pause)
> > (she does a tiger growl)
> Bye bye.

The song Jungle Julia requested comes on the radio.

The girls move and shake to the beat of the song.

Stuntman Mike's car catches up with them...

...And then he passes them...

...Hitting the gas, going even faster so he can pull
ahead and leave them behind.

We cut back and forth between the girls and Stuntman
Mike driving, and Pam, whose nose is smashed; her jaw
is broken and part of her upper teeth are knocked out
but her eyes still work. She watches and pleads to
the driver on the other side of the Plexiglas box.

Then Stuntman Mike makes a U-turn.

The car stops, but the engine runs.

He watches the girls car, far off in the distance,
come forward.

He turns off his headlights.

He revs up the engine.

He hits the gas.

The girls move to the song obliviously.

He heads toward them...

Pam watches in terror.

The other girls are obviously oblivious of what's
about to happen to them.

They continue to chair dance.

His car is almost on them...

Then...

He hits the headlights.

The girls see the car.

He swerves head on into their lane going about a
hundred and thirty.

                    THE MOMENT BEFORE
                       IMPACT

JULIA
with her feet up on the windshield sees the grill of
the car head right for her.

Her face registers.

As she's bathed in harsh, fast-approaching headlights.

LANNA-FRANK
Sees Pam's bloody face directly across from her
heading for a collision.

STUNTMAN MIKE
Lets out a heehaw type of yell, as he heads toward
Julia and her feet.

SHANNA'S
Smile disappears.

ARLENE
Sees Mike's face as she heads toward collision and
softly closes her eyes.

CRASH

As much as we'll show the cars crashing in a horrible
collision, we'll also cut back and forth to what's
happening inside the automobiles.

It'll be a slow motion equivalent of the crash test
dummies footage we've seen before, but with real
people.

The steering wheel is pushed through Lanna-Frank's
chest as she folds around it.

Jungle Julia is propelled feet first through the
windshield—like being shot from a gun out of a shark's
mouth—only to be squashed by the colliding car.

Stuntman Mike's front tires tear into the roof of the
girls' car, and the spinning front tire hits Arlene
square in the face, ripping her face off.

STUNTMAN MIKE
Just enjoys the ride.

Stuntman Mike crashed into the girls on a highway that
was part of an overpass, so the two twisted wrecks
tumble over the side, crashing onto the highway below.

Shanna looks up and sees Stuntman Mike's car falling
on her; she's pulverized.

Another car, also driven by a woman, sees the twisted
cars fall into the road in front of her; it's too late
to do anything.

She crashes into both of them at seventy miles an
hour, destroying her car and herself.

AFTERMATH

The highway is deserted except for the busted cars,
broken glass, blood, flesh, body parts and accident
ravished corpses of the young ladies.

We see a tape put in a tape player.

Mike, alive and well and upside down in his car, comes
down off his rush, as he rocks out to the music.

No one's alive to witness his orgasm, but boy did he
have a good goddamn time.

FADE TO BLACK

FADE UP

INT. HOSPITAL—DAY

We fade up on a hospital door. The door opens, and we see two detectives questioning Stuntman Mike, who's convalescing in a hospital bed.

Texas Ranger EARL MCGRAW walks out of the room; he's joined in the hallway by his son, Texas Ranger EDGER MCGRAW.

                    EDGER
        So, Pop, what'dya think?

                    EARL
        What do I think? Well, son, number
        one, what I think is so ghoulish I
        hesitate to speak it out loud.

                    EDGER
        Give it a shot.

                    EARL
        Well, son, what we got here is a
        case of vehicular homicide. I think
        that ol' boy in there murdered them
        pretty little gals. He used a car,
        not a hatchet, but they dead just
        the same.

                    EDGER
        What are you gonna do?

                    EARL
        Not a damn thing. D.A. says ain't
        no crime here. Every damn one of
        them gals was swimming in alcohol
        and floatin' on weed! "Hooper" in
        there was clean as a whistle.

                    EDGER
        You actually think he
        premeditatedly murdered those
        girls?

                    EARL
        I can't prove it, but since
        thinkin' don't cost nothin', I can
        think it, and I do.

                    EDGER
        Yeah, but, Pop, he got pretty banged
        up hisself?

                    EARL
Yeah, he got banged up. But them
poor girls looked like a giant
chewed 'em up and spit 'em out.

                    EDGER
Why?

                    EARL
I'd guesstamate it's a sex thing,
only way I can figure it. High
velocity impact. Twisted metal.
Bustin' glass. Four souls taken at
exactly the same time. Probably the
only way that diabolical degenerate
can shoot his goo. Only thing we
can even dream of gettin' him on is
vehicular manslaughter for that
hitchhiker in the death box. That
was just plain goddamn reckless
endangerment. But I got me a
bartender owner operator that'll
testify that Stuntman Mike didn't
drink a drop all night. And his
passenger was left stranded by her
date, in the goddamn rain no less,
and she asked him for the ride. On
paper looks like he was just
helpin' her out; that's what a
jury's gonna see anyway.

                    EDGER
So what are you gonna do, Pop?

                    EARL
Well, I could take it upon myself
to continue workin' the case in my
off hours. Keep searchin' for
evidence to prove my theory. Keep
tabs on that bastard. Alert
authorities. Dog 'im.Wherever he
goes, I go. Or...I could spend
that same amount of time and energy
followin' the NASCAR circuit. Now,
I've thought a lot about it, and I
think I'll have a happier life if I
do the latter. But even though I
can't punish Frankenstein for what
he's done, if he ever does it
again, I can make goddamn sure he
don't do it in Texas.

                                    FADE TO BLACK

FADE UP

EXT. HIGHWAY SIGN—DAY

We fade up on a big highway billboard that says
"Welcome to Lebanon, Tennessee."

A SUBTITLE APPEARS on the screen:

                "14 Months Later"

The subtitle fades off.

We look at the sign for a moment...

WHEN
from off screen, a new badass muscle car makes a jump
and CRASHES through the sign.

The car lands on the highway and just keeps on going.

INT. CAR (MOVING)—DAY

Stuntman Mike, back in shipshape, in a brand new Death
Proof muscle car, drives down a Tennessee road,
blaring hillbilly music from the radio, on the hunt.

He pulls the car into a Circle A convenience store
parking lot. He turns the engine off as his tape
player continues.

When...

...in the parking space next to him...

...a car with three girls in their twenties pulls up
in front of the Circle A.

These girls are part of a film crew that is shooting on
location in Tennessee.

Behind the wheel is a pretty black girl with a solid
athletic build, dressed in jeans and a tight green
camouflage t-shirt, named KIM (a stuntwoman).

Beside her, in the passenger seat, is a young pretty starlet, LEE, who by the way just happens to be dressed in a cheerleader uniform. And lying down in the backseat, with her bare feet out the car door window, is the sleeping ABERNATHY (makeup and hair).

It being early dawn, it's obvious these girls have been out partying all night, and have turned into vampires by the early morning light.

Like somebody fascinated would watch pretty, colorful fish through the windows of an aquarium, Stuntman Mike watches his new 3 girls 3 posse through the windows of his automobile.

He watches them talk silently through the window, with only the sound of his tape player's music. He turns off the music and rolls down the window a crack so he can hear them.

>   KIM
>   So are you on the same floor as him?

>   LEE
>   No, I'm on the fourth, and he's on
>   the seventh.

                                        CUT TO

INSIDE THE GIRLS' CAR—MORNING

>   KIM
>   And who's in whose room?

>   LEE
>   He's in mine.

>   KIM
>   And so what happened then?

>   LEE
>   Well, that was pretty much it. We
>   made out in the hall for about ten
>   minutes, then I sent him off to his
>   room.

>   KIM
>   So how's the Rock as a kisser?

>   LEE
>   Oh, he's damn good. He's got them
>   mushy lips, and them fingertips.

KIM
Uuummm, I love them mushy lips.

LEE
And he's a big guy, so he spins me
around.
    (she demonstrates by pantomime)
So my back is up against him, he
takes his big hand, puts it on my
throat, tilts my head back, lowers
over me, and kisses me from behind.

KIM
Damn, that sounds sexy.

LEE
It was sexy.

KIM
But then that was it, you sent him
off? How'd he take it?

LEE
Wait a minute, what are we doin'
here?

KIM
If I'm gonna power through and pick
Zoé up at the airport, I need a
bigass cup of coffee. But finish up
about the Rock; how'd he take it?

LEE
Well, naturally, he tried to talk
me into it.

KIM
What'd he say?

LEE
You know, the whole thing about
let's just sleep together, we don't
hafta do nothin'...

KIM
Yeah, right, nigga, you got ta go.

LEE
But I told him look on the bright
side.

                         KIM
          If there's a bright side ta sending
          a nigga off to his room alone to
          jack off with the soap, I don't know
          that side. What side would that be?

                         LEE
          I told him, if we had sex tonight,
          I'd want to avoid him tomorrow on
          set. Now, the way it stands, I
          can't wait to see him.

                         KIM
          Ooohhh girl, that's a good one, you
          good. So, did you?

                         LEE
          Hell yeah. It was fun smiling at
          him across the set all day.

Kim turns to leave the car, to go into the store and
get her coffee...

                         LEE
          Wait a minute, what time is it?

                         KIM
          Six thirty in the morning.

                         LEE
          You can buy alcohol in the morning
          in Tennessee, can't you?

                         KIM
          If by you, you mean alcoholics, then
          yes, you can buy liquor in the
          morning.

                         LEE
          Shut up. Look, I'm the only one
          here drinks gin, and I drunk the
          last of the gin, last night. So if
          we're gonna party tonight, I need
          me more gin. Bombay, if you please.

                         KIM
          Bombay Sapphire, and tonic, got it.

She opens the door...

                         LEE
          And some Capitol W's Lights.

                    KIM
      Got it.

                    LEE
      And some "Sunny D" if they got it.

                    KIM
      Damn, girl, I just stopped to get
      some coffee, not a pain in the ass.

The sleeping Abernathy pipes in, without getting up or
opening her eyes.

                    ABERNATHY
      Since you're getting that, get some
      more vodka and some more sugar-free
      Red Bull.

The two girls look to the backseat.

                    KIM
      We didn't know you were awake.

                    ABERNATHY
      I'm not awake, I'm asleep, but get
      the vodka and sugar-free Red Bull
      anyway.

They laugh. Kim gets out, then says to Lee:

                    KIM
      You remember how to get to the
      airport, don'tcha?

                    LEE
      Uh-huh.

                    KIM
      Well, then, you should scoot over,
      cause you should drive.

Kim goes, as Lee scoots over to the drivers seat.

INT. STUNTMAN MIKE'S CAR—MORNING

He watches the cute, black girl with the oh so fine
behind walk into the convenience store and do her
business.

His eyes go to the car next to him, Lee in the driver's
seat, pluggin' her iPod earphones into her earholes. And
the two bare feet sticking out of the backseat driver's
side door.

He looks intently.

INT. CIRCLE A STORE—MORNING

Kim is by the cold drinks cooler; she gets the Sunny
Delight, but they don't have sugar-free Red Bull, so
she walks to the front door, opens it, and yells to
the car from where she is.

                    KIM
                 (yelling)
         They ain't got sugar-free Red Bull.
         They got regular Red Bull and
         sugar-free G.O. Juice.

INT. CAR (PARKED)—MORNING

Lee turns to the eyes-closed sleeping beauty reclining
in the backseat.

                    LEE
         I'm aware you're not awake, and not
         to bother you, but they don't have
         sugar-free Red Bull. They've got
         regular Red Bull and sugar-free
         G.O. Juice.

Without opening her eyes, Abernathy says:

                    ABERNATHY
         G.O.

INT. STORE

Kim hears this, gets the G.O. Juice, walks up to the
counter, places the Sunny Delight on the counter, and
asks the guy behind the counter:

                    KIM
         Pull me down a bottle of Bombay
         Sapphire, and Galileo Vodka. And a
         pack of Capitol W Lights, and a
         pack of Red Apple Tans.

The COUNTER GUY pulls down the bottles and the
smokes, as Kim goes over to the coffee area and
proceeds to make a bigass cup of coffee, called The
Big A Cup of Coffee.

INT/EXT. STUNTMAN MIKE'S CAR (PARKED)

Stuntman Mike examines her through his windshield.

His eyes then go to the two bare feet of the sleeping girl propped up on the car door window, and her friend in the driver's seat zoning out on her iPod.

He steps out of his car and approaches the two bare feet. Peering inside, he sees Abernathy, dead to the world.

He glances back at the store. Kim's not looking in this direction, too involved in creating the right mixture for her bigass cup of coffee. Lee, back to him, earphones in her ears, singing along with her iPod.

He looks back to sleeping beauty, and the pretty bare feet he's close enough to touch.

Stuntman Mike removes the black leather glove from his burned right hand. Taking his index finger, he runs it down the bare sole of Abernathy's foot.

He watches her.

She doesn't stir.

He then takes his finger and lightly runs it up her bare sole, from heel to big toe.

CU ABERNATHY
the sleeping woman twitches,...

CU TOES
...and curls her toes quickly, but doesn't wake up.

CU STUNTMAN MIKE
Smiles. He looks toward the store.

The black girl inside still occupied...

...the girl directly in front of him, oblivious, singing out loud to the song on her iPod...

...so far, so good.

Time to press his luck.

He takes his index finger and runs it across her toes.

This makes Abernathy stir and remove her feet from the window.

CU ABERNATHY
Her eyes pop open, and she sits up abruptly...

Stuntman Mike has blasted past and walks around the hood
of his car to his driver side door. He doesn't hurry like
he's guilty and fleeing, but like he's absentmindedly
rushing to his car, and maybe he accidently brushed past
her feet on his way, as well as Lee's elbow that was
sticking out the driver's side car door window.

With ear phones still in her ears, she yells after him:

> LEE
> Excuse you!

She turns around and sees Abernathy sitting up in the
backseat. Lee smiles and removes the iPod from her ears.

> LEE
> Sorry, I didn't mean to give you a
> concert.

> ABERNATHY
> No, it wasn't you. That guy bumped
> into my feet when he walked by.
>> (pause)
> I don't know why, but it kinda
> creeped me out.

Just then Stuntman Mike's muscle car ROARS to life, he
REVS IT UP, vibrating next to the two girls.

Lee smiles and holds up her two fingers, making a small
pinch gesture to Abernathy in the backseat.

> LEE
> Little dick.

She smiles till she looks over at Stuntman Mike (for
the first time) staring back at her, smiling.

Upon seeing his face, her smile fades and she says to
herself:

> LEE
> Holy fuckin' shit.

Her next car door neighbor slams the car into reverse
and peels out of there, layin' rubber out to the road.

> ABERNATHY
> What?

> LEE
> Did you get a load of that fuckin'
> dude?

She shakes her head no.

>
> LEE
>
> He looked like he fell outta an
> ugly tree and hit every branch on
> the way down.

>
> ABERNATHY
>
> Where do you get all these old
> sayings?

>
> LEE
>
> I watched "The Jeffersons" a lot.

Then they notice Kim standing at the store front door,
yelling at them again.

>
> KIM
> (yelling)
>
> Hold on a minute! I gotta take a
> fuckin' piss!

Both Abernathy and Lee smile, saying to themselves
quietly in unison.

>
> ABERNATHY AND LEE
> (quietly to themselves)
>
> That's a little more information
> than we needed, Kim...
> (then yelling back
> to Kim)
> ...But you go right ahead!

Kim does.

>
> ABERNATHY
>
> Well, since I'm up I might as well
> hit the ATM.

INT. STORE

Abernathy gets her money when her phone rings. It's
whistling Bernard Herrmann's theme from "Kill Bill."

>
> ABERNATHY
> (into phone)
>
> Hello.

>
> LEE'S VOICE (OS)
>
> It's me.

Abernathy looks out the window and sees Lee in the car talking to her on her cell phone.

> ABERNATHY
> Miss me?

> LEE'S VOICE (OS)
> I think I might be inside this month's issue of Allure.

She turns toward the Counter Guy.

> ABERNATHY
> Do you have Allure?

> COUNTER GUY
> Magazines by the window, fashion section up top.

TIME CUT

An Allure magazine is tossed on the counter. The Counter Guy rings it up.

> COUNTER GUY
> You know we sell other fashion magazines behind the counter.

> ABERNATHY
> No, that's okay, this'll be all. Thanks a lot anyway.

She turns her back to him and heads for the door...

...when he says to her back:

> COUNTER GUY
> I have this month's issue of Italian Vogue.

...she stops in her tracks...

...then slowly turns her head to look at him.

> ABERNATHY
> This month's?

INT. LEE IN CAR (PARKED)

Listening to her iPod when Abernathy comes out to her. She removes her headphones.

                    ABERNATHY
Okay, listen to this. The Circle A
clerk has this month's Italian
Vogue.

                    LEE
No way?

                    ABERNATHY
Way.

                    LEE
I can't believe this fuckin' Circle
A carries Italian Vogue.

                    ABERNATHY
It doesn't. It's his own personal
copy. He'll let it go for eighteen
bucks.

                    LEE
              (incredulous)
Eighteen bucks?

                    ABERNATHY
What do you care, we're talkin'
about fuckin' per diem here. Look,
we found an issue of Italian Vogue
in Lebanon, Tennessee; we're lucky
he's not asking for fuckin'
Krugerrands. I'm getting it and
we're splitting it three ways.

                    LEE
What, me, you, and Kim?

                    ABERNATHY
No, Kim doesn't give a shit about
Italian Vogue. But Brandy'll come
in with us, and if she won't,
Tyson, her assistant, will.

                    LEE
Okay, but if anybody tears out
any sheets I want, you hafta make
color Xeroxes of those pages. And
I'm not talkin' about no fuckin'
Kinko's either. You go to the art
department and have 'em do it
fuckin' right.

Abernathy, who was leaning into the car to speak with Lee, straightens up to walk back into the store and sees Stuntman Mike's car parked down the road. When she looks directly at it, the automobile speeds away.

This troubles the young lady but she's not sure why.

INT. AIRPORT (TENNESSEE)—DAY

A group of passengers are disembarking from an airplane and filing out into the airport.

Kim, Lee, and Abernathy are watching them disembark, searching for a recognizable face.

Which is what they see when the bouncy, athletic, and cute as a bug's ear Kiwi, ZOÉ BELL, exits the airplane.

Upon seeing the waiting friends, Zoé lights up and bounces over to them, passing out hugs.

It's obvious that while Kim and Abernathy know Zoé, Lee doesn't.

It's also equally obvious that Zoé and Kim are very close, which will make sense when the audience realizes both gals are stuntwomen.

                    ZOÉ
                 (to Kim)
          I see you still wear camouflage to
          all occasions.

                    KIM
          Hey, camouflage is the new black; it
          goes with everything.

After the girlfriends exchange hugs and greetings...

Kim and Abernathy introduce their new location buddy, Lee, to Zoé.

Zoé shakes the actress's hand strongly and vigorously, like a bloke, her New Zealand accent sing-songing a greeting.

EXT. AIRPORT—DAY

From a long distance away, we see the four women, complete with Zoé's baggage, exit the airport.

WE SNAP ZOOM to a medium of Zoé, then a CLICK SOUND off screen and the image of Zoé FREEZES.

Sergio Leone CU of Stuntman Mike observing the girls through the shutter of his camera.

SNAP ZOOM and FREEZE FRAME to each girl in turn.

Stuntman Mike lowers the camera from in front of his face, smiles a shit-eating grin (he's back in business).

> STUNTMAN MIKE
> (to himself)
> Hello, ladies. We're gonna have a good time.

He exits FRAME.

                                        CUT TO

INT. CAR (MOVING)—DAY

The four girls are packed in the car.

> ABERNATHY
> ...Your timing couldn't be better, Zoé. It just so happens, we're all three off duty for the next three days of shooting.

> ZOÉ
> Fuckin' hell; how does that happen?

> ABERNATHY
> Well, I'm doing Lindsay Lohan's makeup, and she's off for the next three days. There's no stunts being filmed during that time, so Kim's free, and Lee's on a will notify for the next four days.

> LEE
> Yeah, but if it rains that'll all change for me; their cover set is the cafeteria scene between me and Brandy.

> ZOÉ
> Brandy, the girl that plays Moesha?

                              KIM
              Oh, hell no. They show Moesha in
              New Zealand?

                              ZOÉ
              Hell, yeah,
                    (she sings the theme)
              "Mo-to-the-E-to-the..."

They all laugh.

                              KIM
              Oh, that's great. Now it's gonna be
              one of them days I can't get the
              Moesha theme out of my head.

                              ZOÉ
              So how's the shoot going?

                           ABERNATHY
              Great. We're having the best time.
              The director, Cecil Evans, is so
              much fun. We're making the coolest
              movie and partying all the time.

The name Cecil is pronounced like Cecil Brown and
rhymes with vessel, not like "Beany and Cecil" and
rhyming with diesel.

                              KIM
              Hell yeah, the next job after this
              is definitely gonna suck.

                              ZOÉ
              So let's hear it, ladies. Set
              romances; who's getting it off?

                              KIM
              That would be Lee and Toolbox.

                              ZOÉ
              Ohhhh, Toolbox, the name sounds
              promising.

                           ABERNATHY
              He's a grip.

                              LEE
              What he is, is a pervert.

                    ZOÉ
          Well, he keeps sounding better and
          better. What's his perversion?

                    LEE
          He likes to watch me pee.

The girls laugh.

Kim and Abernathy chant:

                    ABERNATHY AND KIM
                         (singing)
          Lee's sitting on the toilet and
          Toolbox is watching her pee,
          P-I-SS-I-N-G.

                    KIM
          Yeah, but not no more. Now she's
          gittin' it on with the Rock.

                    ZOÉ
          Your havin' one off with the Rock?

                    LEE
          Not the real Rock. He's a
          electrician named Bruce. But Kim
          calls him the Rock cause he looks
          like the Rock, and now we all just
          call him the Rock.

                    KIM
          Yeah, this is an all-star crew. We
          gotta guy looks like Nic Cage, and
          a guy who looks like Pee Wee Herman
          too.

                    ZOÉ
          Kim — dick department — let's hear
          it?

                    KIM
          No dick this trip. I gotta man.

                    ZOÉ
          Is he coming up every couple of
          weeks and visiting ya?

                    KIM
          Yep,...that's why no dick this
          trip.

The girls laugh.

                         LEE
          Just remember, Kim, whoever you do
          in Tennessee, stays in Tennessee.

                         KIM
          I heard that Niagara Falls.

They laugh.

                         ZOÉ
          How long have you had a boyfriend?

                         KIM
          About three months.

                         ZOÉ
          Who'd you steal him from?

The other girls laugh.

                         KIM
          Nobody.

                         ABERNATHY
          Kim...he totally had a girlfriend.

                         ZOÉ
          All of Kim's boyfriends started out
          as somebody else's boyfriend.

                         KIM
          I didn't steal him. I didn't steal
          any of them...they just...jumped
          ship.

They laugh.

                         ZOÉ
          What's your story, Abernathy?

                         LEE
          Abby's got the big Kahuna.

                         ABERNATHY
          I had a set crush on Cecil.

                         KIM
          Set crush, nigga, please. You were
          his set wife.

                         ABERNATHY
          Were and had being the key words
          here.

                    KIM
         Bitch, you two are still into each
         other and you know it.

                    ABERNATHY
         Oh yeah, well, if he's so in love
         with me, then why did he fuck Daryl
         Hannah's stand-in?

                    KIM
                 (smart ass)
         Because he's a man?

                    ZOÉ
         Yeah, was that a trick question?

                    ABERNATHY
         Yes, men are dogs; oh it's so
         funny, oh it's so funny.

                    KIM
         Oh stop actin' like you all hurt;
         your ass is just mad.

                    ABERNATHY
         Yeah, he's a stand-in fucker.

                    KIM
         Bitch, you need to get over that
         shit, that was two weeks ago.

                    ABERNATHY
                 (sarcastic)
         Oh, well, now you put it like that.

The girls laugh.

                    ABERNATHY
         Oh, I haven't told you the best
         part. He fucked her on my birthday.

                    ZOÉ
         Oh. That's a horse of a different
         color.

                    ABERNATHY
         Thank you.

                    ZOÉ
         Did he know it was your birthday? He
         is the director; he's kinda busy.

                    ABERNATHY
He ate a piece of my birthday cake,
and he got me a present. Yeah, I
think he knew.

                      ZOÉ
What did he get you?

                    ABERNATHY
He made me a tape.

                      LEE
He made you a tape?

                    ABERNATHY
Yeah.

                      LEE
He didn't burn you a CD, he made
you a tape?

                    ABERNATHY
Yes, and I know what you're gonna
say, so don't even go there.

                      KIM
Sounds like the test of true love to
me.

                    ABERNATHY
Look, I know you guys like him,
he's likable. But he fucked another
woman on my birthday. How can you
not be on my side?

                      ZOÉ
Well, I admit that sounds bad.

                    ABERNATHY
It is bad.

                      ZOÉ
It just sounds like a little more
to it than that. Were you two
fucking?

                      KIM
Hell no.

                    ABERNATHY
                    (to Kim)
Hello, is your name Abernathy?

                    KIM
Sorry.

                 ABERNATHY
                  (to Zoé)
The answer to your question is no,
of course not.

                    ZOÉ
What do you mean, "no, of course
not"?

                 ABERNATHY
The reason Cecil hasn't had a
girlfriend in six years is because
girls will fuck him. And if you
fuck Cecil, you don't become one of
his girlfriends — not to say I want
to be his girlfriend — but if I did
want to be his girlfriend, if I
fucked him, I wouldn't be his
girlfriend, I'd be one of his
regulars. And I'm just getting too
fuckin' old for that shit.

                    ZOÉ
How about blow jobs?

                 ABERNATHY
Nope, no blow jobs.

                    ZOÉ
You've at least made out, right?

                 ABERNATHY
Zoé, no. He does that shit with too
many other girls. I'm not going to
be that girl.

                    ZOÉ
You've never even kissed?

                 ABERNATHY
We've kissed.

                    ZOÉ
But no tongue?

                 ABERNATHY
No, no tongue. Not that he hasn't
tried.

                         ZOÉ
Have you let him do anything?

                      ABERNATHY
Yes. I've let him give me a foot
massage, and when we go to the
movies, I've let him hold my hand.

                         KIM
Bitch, you may be actin' like
you're twelve years old, but he's
just actin' like a man. You need to
break that nigga off a piece.

                         ZOÉ
So let me get this straight: you're
not fuckin' em, you're not suckin'
em, you're not giving him any
tongue. But Daryl Hannah's stand-in
is. You know some cultures might
say he made the wiser choice.

                      ABERNATHY
Try being married to a prick who
cheats on you, and see if you're
still singing the same tune.

                         KIM
We ain't talkin' about marriage.
We're talkin' about you and Cecil;
you and Cecil married?

                      ABERNATHY
No.

                         KIM
Marriage is different. When a man
finally breaks down and marries your
ass, he's made the decision to settle
down. That's why niggas try to hold
that shit off to the last possible
minute. Not only that, he's even made
a vow to God, and in front of his
peoples, that he's gonna settle down.
Now how that shit works in the
looong run remains to be seen. For
both y'all. But that's a whole
different thing. But this, I'm your
girlfriend you're my boyfriend Mickey
Mouse mess?

                    KIM
All that means is I got a date on
Saturday night, and on my birthday
and Christmas that nigga better go
deep in pocket. And by the way, what
the fuck are we talkin' about anyway?
You're neither married to Cecil or
his girlfriend. That nigga can do
what he please. Before you can claim
a nigga, you got to claim a nigga.
And you can start by givin' that
motherfucker a hand job in the back
of the van on Tuesday.

                  ABERNATHY
I'm not gonna do that.

                    KIM
I know you won't. But you know who
will, the bitch that <u>ends</u> <u>up</u> livin'
in that bigass mansion of his.

                    LEE
You know, I gotta say, I haven't
entirely agreed on everything Kim
said. But it's true when you stretch
shit out as long as you have with
Cecil. If you suddenly get dirty on
'em, it blows their mind.

                    KIM
Look, baby, I love you, but you
better recognize, Cecil's a good
man. You give him a hand job on
Tuesday, and he'll write your ass a
<u>poem</u> on Wednesday. And when y'all
get married, at your wedding you
give me presents.

Abernathy has stopped arguing and sits back thinking a
bit about what her friend said.

                    KIM
Mark my words, when this movie's
over and done with, them two gonna
get married.

                  ABERNATHY
I'm not gonna marry him.

                    KIM
Mark-my-words!

The girls laugh.

> ABERNATHY
> Okay, can we just take my sex life
> off the table?

> ZOÉ
> Actually, it was Cecil's sex life
> that was on the table and your lack
> of one.

The girls bust up, especially Kim, who does a Sam
Jackson pimp laugh.

Zoé and Kim give a high five.

> ABERNATHY
> Oh, fuck both of you and your
> little high five.

INT. COFFEE SHOP—DAY

> ABERNATHY
> So Zoé, Kim, and I are in the
> Philippines at an outdoor rave.

> LEE
> What were you working on?

> KIM
> "Three Kicks to the Head, Part
> III."

> ABERNATHY
> And, admittedly, we're a little
> fucked up.

> ZOÉ
> Cheers to that.

They all cheers their coffee, and Abernathy continues
her story.

                        ABERNATHY
So Zoé the genius wants to take a
picture of me. It's dark as hell, and
you can't see shit. So she's got her
camera, and keeps saying step back a
little. So I do. Then a little
further. So I step back a little
further. Step back more. So I do,
then I realize I'm right at the edge
of a seven-foot concrete ditch, with
god knows how many rocks and broken
bottles and rats in it. And if I fell
in that, I would've broken my fuckin'
neck. So I'm yelling at her: "Zoé,
you almost killed me." So we
laugh about it, and walk a little
further, and Zoé starts fuckin'
around, and damn if she doesn't fall
in the fuckin' ditch.

The other girls laugh.

Zoé takes their laughter like applause and bows.

                        ZOÉ
I remember taking a step looking
down and just as I'm thinking "Oh,
there's that ditch Abby was talkin'
about," bam, I fall in.

                        LEE
What happened?

                        ABERNATHY
What, with Zoé the Cat? Nothing. If
I fell in that fuckin' thing, they
would of had to helicopter me out
of there. Zoé just lands on her
feet. But then later I started
feeling a little bad about myself.
Zoé falls in the ditch and it's
nothin'. We're laughing about it.
If I fell, I probably would of been
fuckin' paralyzed.

                        LEE
Oh, honey, you can't think like
that. We all have our individual
talents, that just happens to be
one of Zoé's.

                              KIM
          Well, physically speaking, Zoé is
          amazing. I mean agility, reflexes,
          nimbleness, there's few human
          beings that can compete with Zoé on
          that front.

                              ZOÉ
          Awww, Kim, I like you, too.

                              KIM
          Having said that, before you get
          too envious of Zoé's prowess,
          you're missing the most important
          part of that story. You didn't fall
          in the ditch, Zoé did.

The other girls laugh; Zoé acts miffed.

                              KIM
          Zoé even knew there was a ditch
          there, because you told her, and
          she <u>still</u> fell in. So Lee's
          right.We all have our talents.

Zoé acts irate.

                              ZOÉ
          Hey, I resemble that remark.
                    (said like I resent
                    that remark)
          So, Kim, still pack a Roscoe?

                              KIM
          Check it out, bitch.

Zoé bends down and looks under the table.

Kim lifts her left pant leg up, and we see she wears a
pistol in an ankle holster.

                              ZOÉ
                    (impressed)
          Oh, nice one, mate.

                              LEE
          What's a Roscoe?

                              ZOÉ
          A Roscoe's a pistol.

                              LEE
          You carry a gun?

                         KIM
Uh-huh.

                         LEE
Do you have a license to carry it?

                         KIM
                    (sarcastically)
Yeah, when I became a Secret
Service agent, they gave me a
license.

                         LEE
I didn't know you were a —

The other three look at her incredulously...

                         LEE
— I didn't say it. Stop looking at
me. I didn't say it.

                         ZOÉ
That's Kim for ya', always takin'
the piss.

                         KIM
I'm always takin' a what?

                         ZOÉ
Don't hurt yourself, it's Ozbonics,
mate.

                         LEE
                    (to Abernathy)
Did you know Kim carries a gun?

                         ABERNATHY
Yes. Do I approve, no. Do I know,
yes.

                         KIM
Look, I don't know what futuristic
utopia you live in, but the world I
live in, a bitch needs a gun.

                         ABERNATHY
You can't get around the fact that
people who carry guns tend to get
shot more than people who don't.

                    KIM
And you can't get around the fact,
that if I go down to the laundry
room in my building at midnight
enough times, I might get my ass
raped.

                    LEE
Don't do your laundry at midnight.

                    KIM
Fuck that! I wanna do my laundry
whenever the fuck I wanna do my
laundry.

                  ABERNATHY
There's other things you can carry
other than a gun. Pepper spray.

                    KIM
Motherfucker try to rape me, I
don't wanna give him a skin rash. I
wanna shut that nigga down.

                  ABERNATHY
How 'bout a knife at least?

                    KIM
You know what happens to motherfuckers
carry knives...
they get shot. Look, if I ever
become a famous actress, I won't
carry a gun. I'll hire me a
do-dirt-nigga, and he'll carry the
gun. And when shit goes down I'll
sit back and laugh. But until that
day, it's Wild West motherfucker —
                  (to Zoe)
So Zoé, you thought about whatcha'
wanna do first?

                    ZOÉ
It just so happens I know exactly
what I wanna do.

                    KIM
Oh really, and what would that be?

                         ZOÉ
          To me there's no point being in
          America unless you're gonna drive a
          Detroit muscle car. And I want to
          drive a Dodge Challenger, fuck me
          swinging, balls out.

The girls laugh.

                      ABERNATHY
          I guess we can talk to transpo.
          Does it hafta be a Dodge
          Challenger?

                         ZOÉ
          It's got to be a 1970 Dodge
          Challenger with a 440 engine.

The girls bust out laughing.

                         KIM
          And how in the fuck do you expect
          to do that?

                         ZOÉ
          No worries, mate, I got it all
          worked out.

She takes out a local newspaper.

                         ZOÉ
          When I knew I was gonna come here, I
          went on the net and found out the
          local newspaper here in Tennessee is
          the Lebanon News Sentinel. So back
          home —

                         LEE
          — I'm sorry, where's home,
          Australia?

Both Kim and Abernathy wince when Lee says the "A"
word.

Zoé acts mock angry.

                         ZOÉ
          What do you mean by that, mate?

Lee is confused.

Abernathy explains.

                         ABERNATHY
          Zoé's from New Zealand, and you
          never, I repeat never, call a Kiwi
          an Aussie.

                            KIM
          That is unless you want your ass
          kicked.

                            LEE
          Sorry.

                            ZOÉ
          That's okay, I'm just taking the
          piss outta ya. Auckland, to answer
          your question. Anyway, I subscribed
          to the local paper about a month
          ago.

                            KIM
          Now why in the fuck you wanna local
          redneck newspaper in New Zealand?

                            ZOÉ
          Pipe down and I'll tell ya. I've
          been gettin' the paper for the
          last month, and I've been checking
          the classifieds in the back,
          looking at the cars for sale. So,
          as of yesterday, for sale, in this
          town, some guy is selling his
          stock 1970 Dodge Challenger with a
          440 engine, and a white paint job.

                            KIM
          And you wanna buy it?

                            ZOÉ
          Kim, I may be stupid, but I'm not
          bloody stupid. I want to say I
          want to buy it, so he'll let me
          test drive it. A 1970 Dodge
          Challenger with a white paint job,
          that's Kowalski in "Vanishing
          Point," mate, it's a fucking
          classic. If I can get this guy to
          let me drive it without him, I'll
          blow the doors off that bitch.

                    ABERNATHY
What's "Vanishing Point"?

                      ZOÉ
What's "Vanishing Point"? Abby, I'm
supposed to be the illiterate one.
It's just one of the best American
movies ever made.

                      KIM
Actually, Zoé, most girls wouldn't
know "Vanishing Point."

                    ABERNATHY
Excuse me, most girls? What are you
two?

                      KIM
Yeah, well, we're gearheads; of
course we watched it. Y'all grew up
watchin' that "Pretty in Pink" shit.

                      LEE
I like "Pretty in Pink."

                    ABERNATHY
Oh, so you didn't watch John Hughes
movies?

                      KIM
Of course I did, I'm a girl. But I
also watched car shit too.
"Vanishing Point," "Dirty Mary,
Crazy Larry," "Gone in 60 Seconds" —
the real one, not that Angelina
Jolie bullshit.

                      ZOÉ
We have an outdoor theatre in
Auckland that shows "Vanishing
Point", "Big Wednesday", all the
classics.

INT. BARN—DAY

JASPER, the hillbilly who owns the tobacco road
garbage farm (that seems to be the only thing that
grows) that the girls have driven to, opens up the
doors to his barn.

                    JASPER
        There she is.

All four of the ladies take in the off screen sight.
The other two are impressed, but the two motorheads
are gobsmacked.

> KIM
> (to herself with a black
> rhythm)
> Now, that's what I'm talkin' about.

> ZOÉ
> (in her Kiwi rhythm)
> That's what I'm talkin' about.

We see what they see:

A totally bad ass White Dodge Challenger straight out
of the movie "Vanishing Point."

TIME CUT

They pop the hood. We look up at the two girls; they
like what they see.

We see what they see, a beautiful engine that,
gearheads that they are, gets them wet.

Back to the two girls.

> KIM
> This shit's off the fuckin' hook.

> ZOÉ
> Fuckin' legendary, mate.

TIME CUT

EXT. BARN—DAY

Lee, in her short skirt cheerleader uniform, is asleep
in a rusty patio furniture chair. Abernathy sits on
three tires stacked on top of each other.

An ugly dog who looks like he just escaped a Korean
kitchen, walks through the frame.

Zoé and Kim are haggling with Jasper. Zoé says to
Jasper.

> ZOÉ
> If you'll excuse us for a moment,
> I'd like to have a word in private
> with my business associate.

                         JASPER
You ladies take your time.

                          KIM
What are you waiting for? Ask him
to let ya drive it by yourself.

                          ZOÉ
I intend to. But first I need to ask
you somethin'.

                          KIM
What?

                          ZOÉ
If he lets us take it out on our
own, I wanna play Ship's Mast.

Kim's entire demeanor changes.

                          KIM
                        (loud)
Awwww, hell no.

                          ZOÉ
Would you keep it down, big mouth.

                          KIM
Ain't no way I'm doin' Ship's Mast.

                          ZOÉ
Oh, for Christsakes, Kim —

                          KIM
— don't blaspheme.

                          ZOÉ
Sorry.

                          KIM
Now, what did you say after the
last time?

                          ZOÉ
— Look, I know what I said —

                          KIM
— what-did-you-say?

                          ZOÉ
I know I said we shouldn't do this
again —

                         KIM
        Naw, you didn't say, "We
        shouldn't." You said, "We ain't
        ever gonna do that again."

                         ZOÉ
        — But —

                         KIM
        — But, my ass, you said not only are
        we never gonna play Ship's Mast
        again, but ya also said, if you
        ever do what you're trying to do
        now, to not only refuse, but that I
        had permission to physically
        restrain your ass, if necessary.
        Now, did you or did you not say
        that?

Zoé opens her mouth to weasel out of it.

                         KIM
        Naw naw naw naw, answer the
        question, motherfucker, did you or
        did you not say that?

                         ZOÉ
        Yes, I said it — however —

Kim holds up her hand.

                         KIM
        Whatever with your however.

                         ZOÉ
        Look, I know I said it. And I know
        I meant it.

                         KIM
        Damn skippy you meant it.

                         ZOÉ
        But when I said it, I didn't mean
        in America.

                         KIM
        Nigga, please.

                         ZOÉ
        No, really, I meant, we can never
        do Ship's Mast again in New Zealand
        or Australia.

                        KIM
            You are such a liar.

                        ZOÉ
            I know what I said, when I said it.
            But when I said it, I didn't know
            I'd ever come to America. And when
            I said it, if I had known I'd come
            to America and have the opportunity
            to play Ship's Mast on the fucking
            Vanishing Point Challenger, I would
            of added a however...right?

                        KIM
            Okay, oddly enough, I actually
            understood that. However, just
            because you talked yourself into
            some stupid shit doesn't mean I've
            lost my goddamn mind. You need two
            people to play Ship's Mast, and I
            ain't playing.

                        ZOÉ
            I'll be your best friend.

                        KIM
            I don't need me no best friend that
            lives on the other side of planet
            Earth.

                        ZOÉ
            I'll crack your back.

                        KIM
            You'll crack it anyway.

                        ZOÉ
            Of course I would, but now, while
            I'm here, I'll be your back cracking
            slave. Anytime you want it, ya got
            it, you don't even hafta ask for it.
            You can order me to do it. Just say,
            "Bitch, git over here and get busy."

Kim thinks about this a moment...then makes a deal.

                        KIM
            You crack my back, you give me foot
            massages, and after a shower, you
            put moisturizer on my butt.

                          ZOÉ
          Deal.

They shake on it.

The two girls walk over to Abernathy; the sleeping Lee
is in the b.g.

                          ZOÉ
          So we're gonna see if this guy'll
          let us take the car out without
          him. If he does, you stay here with
          Lee, and we'll be back in a bit.

                       ABERNATHY
          What?

                          ZOÉ
          I said we're gonna see if this
          guy'll let us take the car out
          with —

                       ABERNATHY
          — I heard what you said, I just
          can't <u>believe</u> what you said. You
          know, you two got some fuckin'
          balls.

                          ZOÉ
          What?

                       ABERNATHY
          Don't play dumbass with me. I've
          been up all night. I'm still a
          little drunk, <u>and</u> I have a
          hangover. I should be in my hotel
          room asleep, not fucking around
          here on Tobacco Road. But because
          Zoé wanted to drive some fucking
          "Vanishing Point" car, I'm here.
          Now you two got the balls to ask
          me — no, scratch that — tell me I
          gotta make conversation with Tom
          Joad while the cool kids get to go
          out and play? Bullshit on that.

                          KIM
          It ain't like that.

                       ABERNATHY
          Then what's it like, Kim?

>   ZOÉ
> You guys are our collateral. He's
> not gonna go for it if we all go.

>   ABERNATHY
> You know, I really think <u>one</u> human
> being will be collateral enough.

>   ZOÉ
> You're not gonna wanna do what
> we're doin'.

>   ABERNATHY
> What, drive a car?

>   ZOÉ
> We're doin' more than that.

>   ABERNATHY
> What, drive it fast?

>   ZOÉ
> We're doin' more than that.

>   KIM
> Actually, we're paying you a
> compliment, 'cause we're gonna do
> some stupid shit. But that's okay,
> cause we're stunt people; we ain't
> got good sense. But you got good
> sense and anybody with good sense
> ain't gonna wanna do what we're
> doin'.

>   ABERNATHY
> How do you know I don't want to do
> it?

>   ZOÉ
> 'Cause you're a mom.

>   KIM
> Yeah.

                    ABERNATHY
          You know, we're suppose to be this
          big "posse,"
                    (she makes quotes
                    in the air)
          but that's the excuse you guys use
          whenever you want to exclude me
          from something. So what is it you
          two daredevils are doing that I'm
          just so uncool I can't possibly
          understand?

                    ZOÉ
                    (under her breath)
          You know, since we're kinda conning
          this guy, maybe it's best we don't
          go into detail about it while he's
          watchin' us. Besides, he's probably
          not gonna let us do it anyway.

                    ABERNATHY
          Okay, how about this? I'll talk him
          into it. But if I talk him into it,
          I go along.

                    KIM
          How you gonna do that?

                    ABERNATHY
          That's my problem. But don't worry,
          he'll say yes.

                    ZOÉ
          What are you gonna do, blow 'im?

          She makes a face...

                    ABERNATHY
               No!...

          ...face goes away.

                    ABERNATHY
               ...I'm gonna insinuate that Lee's
          gonna blow 'em.

          All three girls bust out laughing. Kim does her Sam
          Jackson pimp laugh.

                    ABERNATHY
               Not really, but let me handle it.
          We got a deal?

                    KIM
          Okay, listen up, mommy. If you're
          gonna hang with the cool kids, you-
          got-to-be-cool. We take you along,
          you don't say shit. You don't even
          say crap. You just sit in the back,
          and I don't wanna hear a peep outta
          your ass. You understand?

Abernathy is happy her cool friends are letting her
play with them.

                    ABERNATHY
          Got it.

                    KIM
          I'm serious now, you start naggin'
          us, we're pullin' over to the side
          of the road, kickin' your ass out,
          and pickin' you up later.

                    ABERNATHY
          Agreed.

                    KIM
          Okay, go work your magic.

Abernathy walks over to the hillbilly.

                    ABERNATHY
          Hello, sir.

She sticks her hand out; he shakes it.

                    JASPER
          Hello.

                    ABERNATHY
          What's your name?

                    JASPER
          Jasper.

                    ABERNATHY
          Hello, Jasper. I'm Abernathy —

                    JASPER
          Aber-What?

                    ABERNATHY
          Abernathy —

She starts to continue...

                    JASPER
          What your first name?

                   ABERNATHY
          That is my first name. —

She starts to continue...

                    JASPER
          What kind of first name is that?

                   ABERNATHY
          I'll tell ya what, just...call
          me Abby.

                    JASPER
          Okay, Abby.

                   ABERNATHY
          Jasper...we were wondering, if
          my friends and I could take the car
          out for a little test drive on our
          own; you know, just to see if we're
          comfortable in it.

                    JASPER
          Why would I do somethin' stupid
          like that?

                   ABERNATHY
          To better sell your automobile.

                    JASPER
          How do I know y'all ain't just
          gonna steal it?

                   ABERNATHY
          Four reasons actually. One, we're
          not thieves. Two, that would be
          rude. Three, we're staying at the
          Days Inn in town, and you can call
          the hotel and check with the
          management we're registered for the
          next month — actually Zoé's not, but
          Kim and I are, so we're totally
          trackdownable —

                    JASPER
          Who's Kim, the colored girl?

                        ABERNATHY
            Yes...Kim <u>would</u> be the girl of
            color. And reason number four — and
            the most important — while we're
            taking the car out for a little
            spin, that'll give you a better
            opportunity to get acquainted with
            our other friend, Lee.

She does kind of a ta-da presentation of the sleeping
Lee.

Jasper looks.

                        JASPER
            Why does she look kinda familiar?

                        ABERNATHY
            That would be because she's a
            famous actress.

She holds up the Allure magazine, opened to Lee's
article.

Jasper takes it, looks at it, then at her, then to
Abernathy.

                        JASPER
            Why she dressed like that?

                        ABERNATHY
            Well, you see, we're making a
            Hollywood movie in town, and it's a
            cheerleader movie, and she's one of
            the cheerleaders.

                        JASPER
            What's a cheerleader movie?

                        ABERNATHY
            A movie about cheerleaders.

                        JASPER
            Is it a porno movie?

Abernathy starts to say no, then changes it to:

                        ABERNATHY
            Yes, it is. But don't mention it;
            she's shy.

                        JASPER
            What's the name of the movie?

                        ABERNATHY
            "Cheer Up in Texas."

                              JASPER
                This is Tennessee.

                              ABERNATHY
                It was cheaper to shoot here. You
                know, not promising anything, mind
                you, but you actually look like
                Lee's last boyfriend. She digs your
                type.

                              JASPER
                What type is that, the no neck
                type?

                              ABERNATHY
                With pretty girls, you never know,
                Jasper.

                              JASPER
                She's asleep.

                              ABERNATHY
                Oh, we'll wake her up.

                                                        CUT TO

INSERT A key is turned in the ignition.

The Challenger ROARS to life.

Waking up the sleeping cheerleader —

The three other girls are in the car.

                              ABERNATHY
                        (yells out the car
                        door window)
                Lee, this is Jasper. Jasper, Lee.
                You two kids stay out of trouble.

Like that old commercial, Kim yells:

                              KIM
                Hey, good lookin', be back to pick
                you up later.

They peel out in a shower of gravel.

Lee looks up at Jasper standing over her.

                              LEE
                Gulp.

EXT. BACKROAD HIGHWAY—DAY

The "Vanishing Point" Challenger drives down the lone country road, cutting through the forest.

Inside are the three girls: Kim behind the wheel, Zoé in the passenger seat, and Abernathy in the back.

Zoé begins preparing for Ship's Mast.

Abernathy asks questions but is told to shut up.

Zoé takes her belt off, and asks Abernathy for hers.

She then wraps both belts around the car door window on both sides.

Then shimmies out of the passenger car door window up onto the Challenger's roof.

A shocked Abernathy starts to say something, and Kim cuts her to the quick.

As Kim speeds down the road, Zoé sits on the roof. She then lowers herself down the windshield onto the hood.

Kim drives looking past Zoé's ass.

Zoé on the hood finds the belt on the passenger side and hangs onto it with her right hand. Then Kim helps her get a hold of the belt on the driver's side...

...then once Zoé has both belts in her hands, she lowers on her back all the way down the hood, till her knees are over the hood, and her heels rest on the fender...

Then with her arms stretched out, and her legs spread eagle, lying flat on the Challenger's hood like a human hood ornament, or a...Ship's Mast."

She nods her head forward...

...which is Kim's cue to punch it...

The muscle car speeds down the road with the crazy Kiwi on the hood, laughing her ass off...

                                                        CUT TO

CU STUNTMAN MIKE WITH BINOCULARS
he lowers the specs from his face. This is as close to
flabbergasted as Stuntman Mike ever gets, and the cause
of his flabbergastation is the two badass stuntchicks
who apparently like to play as rough as he does.

He looks around...

...The girls know how to have an uninterrupted good
time...There's nobody around. They are in the middle
of a vast Nowheresville.

Stuntman Mike climbs in his car and starts her up.

She ROARS to rumbling life.

He buckles all his buckles, as...

...his foot revs the gas.

When he's safe and secure, one hand goes to the
gearshift and the other to the wheel...and...

...He takes off after them.

Back tires kicking up grass and sod as the tires spin
to life, before connecting with asphalt.

Once she hits the highway, she straightens out and
power-swims like a shark. Rubber to road like a fin
through the water.

THROUGH THE WINDSHIELD
Coming up fast behind the girls' car.

THE GIRLS' CAR
The trio are oblivious.

ZOÉ
is laughing in daredevil ecstasy.

KIM
is caught up in the adrenaline.

ABERNATHY
can't believe what the fuck she's seeing, but after
being frightened, she's slowly starting to let go and
enjoy the moment. Her shocked mouth slowly turns into
a smile.

STUNTMAN MIKE
So does his.

The grill of his car coming up fast.

ABERNATHY
Something makes her look behind her.

ABBY'S POV
Stuntman Mike's badass muscle car, coming at her at
one hundred and twenty miles an hour.

ABERNATHY
recognizes "Death Proof" as the same car from the
party store, and realizes in the next breath they will
collide.

                    ABERNATHY
                  (to herself)
          Oh my God.

KIM'S
Eye goes up to the rearview.

REARVIEW MIRROR
Car speeding to ram from behind.

                      KIM
          What the fuck —

Stuntman Mike's grill CRASHES into the girls' ass...

...BAM!

Stuntman Mike's car hits them with such force, that
Abernathy is propelled from the backseat, through the
space in the front seat between the driver and
passenger seats, crashing hard into the dashboard.

ZOÉ
feels the car lurch and shake, but doesn't let loose
of the belts.

STUNTMAN MIKE'S
foot presses the brake.

We see from his windshield, we see the girls' car shoot
ahead.

KIM
sees in the rearview mirror the car fall back.

STUNTMAN MIKE'S
foot hits the gas.

His car shoots forward, heading for another crash on
the girls' ass.

KIM
watches it in the rearview. Waiting for impact.

STUNTMAN MIKE
yeehawing, waiting for impact.

CRASH!

Zoé's hand is jerked loose from one of the belts.

As she starts to slide off the hood, she quickly flips over on her belly, and grabs the frame between the hood and the windshield, like a cat on a tree.

ZOÉ
looks up and locks eyes with Kim.

                    ZOÉ
          What the fuckin' hell!

Then she sees what's up. Stuntman Mike's car starts to pull alongside the girls' car.

He swerves his car into theirs.

Zoé is literally yanked from her perch, and does a one eighty twirl and slide. She's now facing the opposite way, head toward the grill, feet toward the windshield. With no hand hold per se, she begins to slowly slide toward the grill.

KIM AND ABERNATHY
in the front seat watch in horror, but there's not a goddamn thing they can do.

STUNTMAN MIKE
sees it too. He knows the next hit will be the death blow, and he wants it to be just right. So he falls back much farther this time.

KIM
sees this, she knows what's coming.

STUNTMAN MIKE
hits the gas.

SPEEDOMETER
jumps.

KIM
he's coming up fast in the rearview.

She has no choice...She's got to out race him.

She hits the gas...

and the chase is on.

ZOÉ
wind in her face, is trying to stop the slide, but she
keeps inching closer to the edge...

KIM
is doing the driving of her life, keeping the car
steady so as not to shake Zoé and still keep ahead of
Mike's car.

Kim screams to Abby:

                    KIM
          Get my gun, it's on my left foot.

As we cut back and forth between the two cars...

...Abby tries to reach the gun, but can't do it as Kim
drives without fucking her up.

                    ABERNATHY
          I can't!

                    KIM
          Fuck!

STUNTMAN MIKE
finds himself in a different situation. Both cars may
look badass, but the girls' Challenger has more under
the hood than his.

And Kim just may be a better driver. He's chasing after
her; he's on her ass, but he can't quite catch her to
smash her.

ZOÉ
has now reached the end of the hood...

...she sees the asphalt of the highway speeding
under her.

She grabs hold of the hood ornament with one hand; as
her upper body begins to fold over the side, she braces
herself by pushing against the fender with her other
hand, thus stopping her slow slide.

Will she continue sliding off? No. Is her position
precarious as hell? Yes. Will a slight bump send her
over the side? Hell, yeah!

ABERNATHY
both hands out in front, bracing themselves on the dash,
a little blood trickling from her scalp, is literally
petrified, with her front row seat view of Zoé hanging
half on, half off their car as it goes eighty miles an
hour.

Suddenly the paved road opens up into a big clearing.

A barn is off to the side. A pile of rubbish. And a
big field of tall grass.

It opens up so wide that Stuntman Mike can get beside
the girls and clips them on their left side.

The Dodge Challenger SPINS OUT like a steel and chrome
muscle dreidel, whipping around a full three
revolutions.

Zoé is sent flying from the hood.

TALL GRASS
Zoé, as if shot from a gun that uses New Zealand women
as ammo, sails over the grass, finally crashing deep in
the brush. Her fall is obstructed from view.

The Challenger skids to a stop. For a moment the
girls sit, shell-shocked.

Stuntman Mike has stopped too. He looks at the girls.
He's thinking maybe he should let these girls be.

When Kim turns and sees him and his car stopped, she
yanks the pistol out of her ankle holster, brings it
up, and FIRES at him.

The bullet hits him right in the shoulder. He screams
at the explosion in his body.

Like a cowardly dog, he hits the gas and drives off.

Both girls look straight ahead, their windshield
pointing directly at the tall grass, their hearts
ready to explode over their friend's fate.

When...

...Zoé's figure, way in the background, leaps up for a
moment above the grass, and she says:

                    ZOÉ
        I'm okay.

KIM AND ABERNATHY
both break out in relieved laughter.

Abernathy rolls her eyes, putting her hands up in
the air.

                    ABERNATHY
          Of course she is. What was I
          thinking!

Zoé walks out of the grass and up to the girls.

                    ZOÉ
          Whew! Now, that was a close one.

                    KIM
          Bitch, you like to give me a heart
          attack.

                    ZOÉ
          Where's the fuckin' maniac?

                    KIM
          I shot his ass and he sped off.

Kim and Zoé look at each other.

                    ZOÉ
          Wanna catch 'em?

                    KIM
          Hell, yeah!
               (she turns to Abernathy)
          Get out, honey.

                    ABERNATHY
          Fuck that, let's kill this bastard.

Zoé sees something.

                    ZOÉ
          Wait a minute.

She runs over to the junk pile and pulls out a heavy-
duty piece of pipe, then hops in the back.

Kim speeds off after Mike.

STUNTMAN MIKE
stops his car. He's bleeding and hurting worse. He's
been shot in the left shoulder, so he can't move his
left arm. With his right hand he unbuckles his straps,
wincing and grimacing with each movement.

He struggles with his right arm to get at his glove box.

He finally does and takes out a bottle of Four Roses
whiskey. He spins off the cap with his thumb and
takes a big down-the-hatch swig.

As the neck of the bottle is in his mouth, his eyes go
to the rearview mirror, and he sees Kim's Challenger
heading at his stopped car at full speed...before he
can remove the bottle...

...BAM!

No longer held tight by the restraints, his face
smashes into the steering wheel with the bottle in the
middle.

Everything but the steering wheel shatters.

The car is sent flying.

Stuntman Mike screams in agony.

With his face smashed and bleeding, with glass
sticking out of his face and neck, he sees Kim
starting her stalled car to ram him again.

He frantically starts his car and peels out in fleeing
terror.

The girls are hot on his trail.

GIRLS' CAR
in hot pursuit. Zoé in the back says:

> ZOÉ
> I've got an idea, Abernathy, give
> me that belt.

Abernathy does.

Zoé starts wrapping it around her waist.

Chase back and forth.

Once the belt's on:

> ZOÉ
> Abby, I need you to get in the
> back.

She does.

>   ZOÉ
>   Now, Kim, I need you to pull up
>   alongside of him on your side, then
>   pull ahead of him, but keep to his
>   right!

Kim starts doing this.

STUNTMAN MIKE
sees the girls' Challenger, moving up alongside of him
on the right.

The two cars are parallel.

Kim and Stuntman Mike share a look. Roles reversed,
he's scared and shaken; she's the cat playing with the
mouse.

The girls' car pulls ahead.

>   ZOÉ
>   Now when I tell ya, hit the brake, got it?

>   KIM
>   Got it.

Zoé opens the backseat car door.

>   ZOÉ
>   Hit it!

Kim's foot stomps on the brake.

The tires lock.

STUNTMAN MIKE
sees he's heading right for the back car door...

...WHAM...

...he takes it right off clean as a whistle.

Zoé, who now hasn't any backseat car door, says to
Abernathy:

>   ZOÉ
>   Now, Abernathy, I need you to hold
>   on to the back of my belt for dear
>   life. Can you do that?

>   ABERNATHY
>   Yes.

                              ZOÉ
            Don't say yes if you can't do it.

                           ABERNATHY
            You're not going anywhere, mate.

                              ZOÉ
            That's what I wanna hear.

Picking up the lead pipe, she says to Kim:

                              ZOÉ
            Now, Kim, I need you to get me
            parallel with his back tire.

Kim pulls up alongside of him.

Zoé, with the pipe raised like a whale harpoon.
Abernathy with one hand holding onto Zoé's belt, and
the other arm wrapped around the seat.

The spinning back wheel of the Stuntman's car comes
into FRAME next to the open backseat doorway.

                              ZOÉ
            You ready, Abby?

                           ABERNATHY
            Ready.

Zoé HARPOONS the pipe into the wheel well, then quickly
lets go.

Stuntman Mike's right back tire locks up, and his tail
goes up in the air, and he FLIPS END OVER END down the
highway, smashing the fucking shit out of the car.

Kim stops the car, and the girls watch the show.

INSIDE VEHICLE
Stuntman Mike, now with an immobile right arm, and no
longer wearing his seat belts, is tossed around the
cab, BUSTING, CRASHING, and SMASHING into everything.

When the car finally stops, it's upside down.

Inside the wrecked vehicle, Stuntman Mike isn't dead,
but he's totally busted, broken, and helpless.

CU STUNTMAN MIKE
upside down. He sees, in upside down vision, the girls'
stopped car. Then he sees the doors open; then he sees
the three girls feet climb out of the car and hit the
pavement.

Then he sees the three pair of feet walk toward him.

He's completely helpless.

They jerk his driver's side door open and roughly yank his busted-up ass out of the vehicle.

Yanking him up onto his feet, while pounding music blares on the soundtrack, the three girls, with their fists, beat him to death.

When he hits the red asphalt, Stuntman Mike is no more.

Once he hits the ground, with the three girls standing over him...

The FILM FREEZE FRAMES like an old school Kung Fu film that ends at the death blow.

A cheesy white optical "The End" pops up on the screen.

And without anymore to do, "Death Proof" is over.